A Throne of Fire

A Shade of Vampire, Book 40

Bella Forrest

Also by Bella Forrest:

THE GENDER GAME

The Gender Game (Book 1)

The Gender Secret (Book 2)

The Gender Lie (Book 3)

The Gender War (Book 4)

The Gender Fall (Book 5)

A SHADE OF VAMPIRE SERIES:

Series 1:
Derek & Sofia's story:

A Shade of Vampire (Book 1)

A Shade of Blood (Book 2)

A Castle of Sand (Book 3)

A Shadow of Light (Book 4)

A Blaze of Sun (Book 5)

A Gate of Night (Book 6)

A Break of Day (Book 7)

Series 2:
Rose & Caleb's story:

A Shade of Novak (Book 8)

A Bond of Blood (Book 9)

A Spell of Time (Book 10)

A Chase of Prey (Book 11)

A Shade of Doubt (Book 12)

A Turn of Tides (Book 13)

A Dawn of Strength (Book 14)

A Fall of Secrets (Book 15)

An End of Night (Book 16)

Series 3:
Ben & River's story:

A Wind of Change (Book 17)

A Trail of Echoes (Book 18)

A Soldier of Shadows (Book 19)

A Hero of Realms (Book 20)

A Vial of Life (Book 21)

A Fork Of Paths (Book 22)

A Flight of Souls (Book 23)

A Bridge of Stars (Book 24)

Series 4:
A Clan of Novaks

A Clan of Novaks (Book 25)

A World of New (Book 26)

A Web of Lies (Book 27)

A Touch of Truth (Book 28)

An Hour of Need (Book 29)

A Game of Risk (Book 30)

A Twist of Fates (Book 31)

A Day of Glory (Book 32)

For an updated list of Bella's books, please visit her website:
www.bellaforrest.net

Join Bella's VIP email list and she'll personally send you an email reminder as soon as her next book is out! Visit here to sign up:
www.forrestbooks.com

Contents

The "New Generation" Names List

- **Arwen:** (daughter of Corrine and Ibrahim - witch)
- **Benedict:** (son of Rose and Caleb - human)
- **Brock:** (son of Kiev and Mona – half warlock)
- **Grace:** (daughter of Ben and River – half fae and half human)
- **Hazel:** (daughter of Rose and Caleb – human)
- **Heath:** (son of Jeriad and Sylvia – half dragon and half human)
- **Ruby:** (daughter of Claudia and Yuri – human)
- **Victoria:** (daughter of Vivienne and Xavier – human)

Tejus

We had ridden hard, pushing the bull-horses to their breaking point, attempting to put as much distance as we could between whatever evil was erupting in the cove and what remained of our sentry forces. The Acolytes had fought ferociously, killing ten of our men before all of them eventually lay slain on the sand. With Queen Trina dead, it was the end of the cult. But they had done their work; the entity was rising, and so was its army. We had learned nothing of any use—we knew nothing of the entity's plans, or what mysterious creatures would rise to ravage our lands.

Our army, though mostly intact, was subdued. We had rescued the children, and Queen Trina's reign was over, but greater dangers were still to come. Fear settled over the sentries of the five kingdoms, dampening any jubilation we might have felt over our small victory. A few guards and ministers had been sent on to the summer palace to retrieve the wounded we had left there. They would re-join us at Queen Memenion's home to get the care and attention they needed. Abelle would be left there, chained, until we knew what to do with her – now the Acolytes were dead, and Jenus was with us, Ash and I felt that it would be the best place for her. Maybe give her time to reflect on what she had done.

Hazel sat in front of me on the bull-horse. Her fingers were clasped tightly around mine, her head resting against my chest. I still couldn't believe that she had been the one to end Queen Trina's life. Nevertide, and I, had a lot to thank her for. If the land survived what was coming, no doubt Hazel's name would be written time and time again in the annals of its history—the courageous girl who had ended the life of its most powerful and evil ruler.

I bent low to gently kiss the crown of her head, noticing how cold her skin felt, how small and fragile she felt to me, even after all she had done to prove she was anything but. Hazel had saved my life, in more ways than one.

"Tejus, look at the sky," Hazel breathed softly. "It's amazing."

Her voice sounded dozy, like she was half asleep. I suspected it was the adrenaline finally leaving her body, and the fact that she hadn't syphoned off anyone in a while.

"It's certainly something," I replied, looking up to the sky. After the last wave of tremors that shook the earth while we were at the cove, the sky had ripped further. Now Nevertide seemed cast in an eternal twilight, half the sky the pale pinks and golds of the setting sun, and half of it midnight black. The strange light threw long shadows, stretching and distorting the shapes of the sentries who rode alongside us.

"You can syphon off me, if you need to. We have Jenus riding at the back as well," I reminded her. I wasn't sure why she wasn't using me or any of the other sentries. She also seemed perfectly content with our physical closeness. Normally she would have withdrawn in hunger by now.

"I don't think I need to…honestly, I just want to sleep. I feel like I could sleep for a hundred years." She yawned, accidentally emphasizing her point. Perhaps it was the adrenaline, then.

"So, sleep," I replied. "I'll wake you when we get there."

"Where are we going?" she asked.

"We're going to Memenion's kingdom. There isn't enough space at the summer palace, and it lacks protection. I doubt we can hide from whatever creatures are going to erupt from the sea, but at least we can ensure that we're heavily guarded until we work out what we're going to do."

She fell silent for a while, and I thought she must have dropped off to sleep, but a moment later she spoke again.

"I know it was the right thing to do, but I feel…strange. I killed somebody." Her voice wavered. "I killed a person."

I wrapped my hand more tightly around hers, my body tensing.

"There was little left of Queen Trina that wasn't evil, Hazel. She would have destroyed all of us—you especially, given half a chance."

"I know," she murmured.

I knew whatever I said wouldn't make her feel any better. It pained me that Hazel would have that on her conscience for the rest of her life—that I couldn't take the burden from her.

"I was only young when I first killed a man," I replied hoarsely. I didn't want to tell her the story—I didn't want her to think any less of me, but it was necessary to let her know she wasn't alone.

"The Thraxus kingdom orchestrated an uprising against my father, wanting to end the imperial rule of the Hellswans. We went to battle. It was short and bloody. Many died. The man I killed was almost twice my age—he had gained on my father, syphoning him strongly. I did what I had to do—what I thought was right. I will never forget the way it felt…I will never forget his face."

I waited for her revulsion, glad that I couldn't see her

expression.

"Tejus," she whispered.

Instead of the condemnation I was expecting, Hazel lifted our linked hands to her lips, pressing a kiss against my fingers.

"It must have been horrible."

I shrugged, hardly believing that she wasn't going to judge me, that my actions weren't repulsive to her.

"It was necessary. Take comfort that Queen Trina was truly evil—not just a man fighting for what he believed was right."

"I guess so," she replied with a sigh.

"Think of your brother, the pain that she caused him—and Ruby and Julian too. They were lucky to survive the ordeals she put them through."

"And the pain she put you through. Commander Varga. The king of Hadalix. So many," she replied, her voice sounding stronger. I started to feel a small flicker of energy radiating off her, and smiled to myself in the darkness. Hazel was so much more resilient than I gave her credit for—she would overcome this, and whatever else we would face in the coming days.

"Rest, Hazel," I commanded her gently. "While we have the time."

I felt her nod against me, and another yawn erupted. Soon her body lay back against mine limply, and I heard the faint, regular breathing of her sleep.

We were a few miles from Memenion's castle. I looked

toward Queen Memenion and Ragnhild, both riding up front. Ash and Ruby had ridden back through the ranks to check on Jenus and were yet to return.

I hadn't decided what we were going to do with my brother yet. I wanted him locked away, but so far any attempt we'd made to keep hold of captives had failed dismally—with near-disastrous results. We still had Abelle locked up and chained in the summer palace. Would we leave her there to die? Or could she be of use to us? From what Hazel had told me of the conversation she had overheard in the forest between the woman and the Acolyte, it didn't seem like Abelle knew much. Perhaps it would be better to leave her to her own fate. No doubt Ash would have an opinion on the matter.

I heard his bull-horse galloping up alongside the army.

"Your brother's still confined," Ash informed me, slowing down to a trot to keep pace alongside me. Ruby sat behind him, smiling softly at Hazel's sleeping form.

"Is he saying anything?" I asked.

"The usual—how put upon he's been, how Queen Trina was evil incarnate and he's just an innocent."

I snorted with derision.

"I don't believe a word he says either." Ash smiled wryly.

"Does he know she is dead?"

Ash nodded. "What do you think we should do with him?" he asked after a pause.

"That's what I'm trying to work out."

"If what the book said is true, that the Acolytes could communicate with the entity, we need to be careful that Jenus can't do the same – who knows to what extent Queen Trina involved him in her plan. He denies it, which is to be expected. It just worries me that if we take him with us, he might be able to impart information to the entity—things that could be used against us."

The words of the book had slipped my mind. If the book was correct, then perhaps we could use it to our advantage.

"Or, if he had fully pledged his allegiance to the Acolytes during his stay with Queen Trina, we could use Jenus's visions to get information about the entity – what he's planning," I countered. "I don't believe for a moment that we will be able to protect ourselves from an attack by the entity at its full strength, no matter how well protected we are. Our best chance of survival will be to understand what exactly it wants, and try to stay one step ahead."

"Does it even want anything?" Ruby asked quietly. "Doesn't it just want us all dead, and Nevertide destroyed?"

"Perhaps," I agreed. "Though I still don't believe that its rise is complete yet—I think we would know if it was."

"We would all be dead already," Ash muttered.

We fell silent. It was the truth. There must be something that the entity was missing, or some process that hadn't been completed yet. Had the book been more forthcoming, we might have a better idea as to what that was—but we were clueless.

"The guards have blindfolded him. Hopefully that will keep our location and our numbers hidden for as long as possible," I said. "There will be ways of making Jenus talk."

Ash looked over at Hazel, still fast asleep.

"At least she'll have a steady supply of energy."

"Is she feeling any better?" Ruby asked, her voice barely above a whisper to avoid waking her friend.

"I think it's the adrenaline that's making her tired. She seems more in control of her hunger though."

Ruby nodded.

"It would be great if she could get that under control—*without* any more potions."

"Perhaps with Jenus's *help* she can."

We stopped talking as the road took a sharp turn, joining the smaller pathway that led up toward Queen Memenion's kingdom. It had been a long time since I'd visited the castle, and it struck me as faintly ironic that we'd be returning to the original birthplace of the Acolytes.

I looked over at the queen. Her eyes were fixed on the castle in the distance, her face as determined as when we'd ridden into battle. I wondered how she felt returning home knowing that her son and husband were dead. I had recognized the face of Ronojoy among the group of Acolytes whose bodies now stained the shoreline, and hoped that she hadn't seen him. She would know soon enough either way, but no mother should have to witness that, no matter what her son had done.

DEREK

We had left the cove behind, stumbling over black-hooded bodies on the shore without taking a moment to discover who or what they were. There hadn't been time. We could all hear the cracking of the stones behind us. A strange sensation had started to prick at the back of my neck that I couldn't quite put into words, aside from the fact that I felt we were being watched, that some great force was awakening from the depths of the ocean, its glare fixed greedily upon us.

"Did you feel that?" Sofia asked me as we reached the mainland.

I nodded. None of us knew what we were up against in this strange land, what creatures would be following us or watching from the tall thickets of trees that surrounded our group as we hurried away from the portal.

Sofia and I ran on, the rest of GASP running or flying low behind us. Soon we reached a clearing, and with the strange sensation having faded almost completely, I decided that now was as good a time as any to regroup. I came to a halt.

"Do you think it's safe to stop here?" my son asked.

"I'm not sure. I want to keep following the army, but I don't want us in a position where we've got enemies both ahead and behind us. Jeriad, Lethe, will you take the other dragons and follow the army that went on ahead? Don't get too close—I don't want them to know we're here, I just want to know *what* they are and where they're headed."

I could have sent Ben and Sherus to ensure that we weren't seen, but I felt like the dragons would be more content if they were able to stretch their wings and get a good look at the landscape. Plus, I needed the fae down on the ground; if we heard creatures approaching up ahead, I would want Ben, Sherus and his sister to thin themselves and go ahead to investigate.

Jeriad's aquamarine eyes fixed on mine.

"They have flying creatures of their own, I'm sure of it. I saw them at a distance."

"Birds," Lethe confirmed. "They looked like vultures to me, but much larger."

Rose looked at the ice dragon with curiosity. "Then they're likely the kidnappers of the children—it's how we think they traveled out of the portal," she muttered. I could see my daughter was desperate to ask the dragons to fly closer, to see if there was any evidence of my grandchildren, but held back—it would only endanger their safety at this stage.

"Recon mission only, Rose," I asserted before she could change her mind.

She nodded, looking sideways at Caleb. Their anxiety was painfully evident, and I wasn't immune to it either. This land was hostile, and I had only a small hope that the children of The Shade would have survived it intact.

"The rest of us need to find shelter. If the creatures emerging from those stones are coming after us, I don't want us left defenseless and out in the open."

"We're hardly defenseless," Claudia retorted, baring her fangs.

I gritted my teeth at her obstinacy.

"We don't know what these creatures are or if we can even kill them. I don't want half of GASP wiped out just because we were uninformed and ill-prepared," I bit back.

Her brown eyes flashed, but she remained silent.

"Let's get out of this forest then," Lucas muttered. "I don't like it… I feel like the trees are watching me."

Lucas articulated what we'd all been thinking—but my

brother in particular had an excuse to fear unknown forests, given his experience in The Dewglades. I looked out into the endless forest, trying to ignore the growing weariness that was creeping up within me again. I wondered which direction we should be heading in. I wasn't sure that following the army would be such a good idea for the rest of us—not yet, anyway.

Jeriad, Lethe and the rest of the dragons had transformed already. Jeriad spread his wings and shot up – hovering just above the tops of the trees. He circled the area, staying low enough to remain out of sight. A few moments later he swept back down to the forest floor.

"Head west," Jeriad said, "there's something there—ruins mostly, like the rest of the land, but it should provide some cover. The sky's been ripped over it as well, so it's as if it's night there. There won't be any need to cast a spell of darkness for the vampires." Jeriad turned to Ibrahim, who nodded.

"Let's get going then," I commanded the rest of the team. "We stick together." The dragons flew up and out of sight. I could have asked the witches to transport us, but they didn't know this land any better than I did – without prior knowledge of the destination, I felt it was too risky. The rest of us headed out, grouping together as tightly as we could. Everyone was unnerved by the strange silence of the land. We were in the depths of a large forest, and yet I couldn't sense or hear a single living thing.

"Look at this," River said. She and Ben were slightly ahead, looking down at the forest floor. I joined them, seeing a small crack in the earth that grew wider as it jaggedly cut the forest floor in an eastern line.

"They must have had an earthquake," River remarked, bending down to touch the edge of the crack. "The soil hasn't been dried out—this was fairly recent."

"It would explain why Jeriad saw ruins. Perhaps the land's been heavily hit by natural disasters?" my son questioned uneasily.

I raised an eyebrow at him.

"Natural or unnatural? Nothing feels quite right here," I replied.

We both looked up at the torn sky. No—nothing felt natural about this place. Whatever had happened here was the result of malevolent forces…something dark and deadly that held this land in its grip.

"Let's keep going. The sooner we reach those ruins the better."

I urged the team on, and soon the density of the forest started to give way to dry earth and a clear pathway out of the trees. Oddly-shaped hoof prints trampled the dirt. It was obviously a popular thoroughfare. I was still looking at the strange markings when a shout went up.

"What's that?" Lawrence called out, gesturing us over to the side of the path, pointing back out into the trees.

"It looks like a colosseum," Grace replied, heading off the path toward the structure.

"Grace, stop!" I ordered. I made my way to where my half-fae granddaughter and her husband were standing, my eyes lighting on the strange stone building off in the distance. From here, I couldn't see an entrance to the building, though whatever it was had remained intact—none of its stonework had been damaged during the earthquake.

"We need to keep going. If the place that Jeriad directed us to is inhabitable, we might return here, but I want us out of the forest."

"Okay," Grace agreed quickly, wrapping her arms around herself. She looked up at me with her turquoise eyes. "I think you're right—let's get out of this place."

We carried on along the path, all of us sighing with relief when we finally left the dark and oppressive shadows of the trees. Corrine fell into step beside me.

"We need to put barriers up as soon as we're settled." The witch spoke in a hushed voice, perhaps careful not to alarm some of the younger GASP members. "Mona, Ibrahim and I have been trying to get a sense of what this...*thing* is that we can all feel, but nothing is revealing itself. At first I thought it might be shrouded in some kind of magic, but we can't sense any witchcraft. We have no idea what this is, and that worries me."

"I know," I replied. "It worries me too. But we've faced the unknown before, Corrine. We just need to make sure that we're being careful. The barriers are a good idea. As soon as we're settled get the rest of the witches on it—I don't want any surprises."

She nodded, hurrying back to Ibrahim and Mona.

The ruins that Jeriad had seen were the remains of a castle. The outer walls were still standing, with the path leading up to a portcullis, the drawbridge lowered and abandoned. The rest of the castle had been completely destroyed—black smoke was still billowing in places from beneath the gray rock, and hardly any of the foundation remained intact.

"This doesn't look too promising," Nuriya stated, surveying the dead lands that lay before us.

"Agreed," Aiden grunted.

I looked back at the rest of the group. Sofia glanced over at me, her eyes wide. It wasn't ideal, but, at the moment I still believed it was the best option we had—it was out of the forest at least.

"Let's explore," I announced, wanting to get the barriers up as soon as possible. "We can find somewhere to camp, at least."

"Are you kidding?" Lucas retorted. "This place could collapse at any moment."

"It already has. Some of the castle still might be habitable. Everyone spread out!"

The group splintered off, the jinn sticking together, and the werewolves and witches doing the same. Rose and Caleb joined the rest of the parents—Landis, Ashley, Claudia and Yuri. Kiev and his family headed straight for the main keep of the castle, to the ruins where the entrance would have been, Brock's arms half-outstretched like the rest of the witches', trying to sense what had come this way before us. Sherus and his sister waited uneasily by the portcullis, more timid than the rest of us about venturing toward the castle.

"Wait!" Micah's wife Kira called out to Rose before she could walk off. "I think I can smell the kids—over here."

In a flash, my daughter was by the werewolves, standing by a fallen tower to the right of the main castle. Sofia and I, and the rest of the GASP members joined them.

"You're right—they were here!" Rose exclaimed, clutching at Caleb's shirt in excitement.

"Actually, the whole place smells of them. They spent a long time around this castle…" Micah started to sniff around, shoving his blond hair away from his face as he tried to get a better scent. Suddenly, he pulled back in disgust. "And the dead. A lot of creatures died here…"

I had thought I'd smelt burning flesh. It made sense—if there had been inhabitants within the castle when it had started to fall, it would have been nearly impossible to get them out.

"But not your kids," Micah hastened to add as he caught the

expression on my daughter's and Sofia's faces. "They're still alive—when they left this place, they were still alive."

Rose nodded slowly, and I could hear her heart rate returning to normal.

"What kind of creatures were the others?" I asked the werewolves.

"Part human for sure." Bastien spoke up. "There's something else in there too…but I can't understand what it is—something we've never come across before."

The werewolves continued to roam through the ruble and debris of the castle, stopping short when they reached Kiev. He and Erik were lifting the stone arches that would have once held up the entrance. The werewolves started to back away in disgust. The reek of burnt flesh hit me full force.

"Wait here," I muttered to Sofia, indicating that she should watch Rose—make sure our daughter and the other parents didn't come any closer. Even though the werewolves had assured us that the kids had left here alive, I didn't want to take any chances.

"They've been roasted beyond recognition," Kiev growled, throwing a stone down in disgust. "Whatever creatures these were, they all died trying to get out of here. Some by falling rock, some later by carbon monoxide poisoning."

I nodded, looking down at the body he'd revealed—or what was left of it. The face had been burnt away completely, and the only noticeably non-human aspect about the figure was its height—the body was freakishly tall.

"They're all like that." Kiev gestured to the rest of the bodies he'd unearthed. "Tall. Human faces, though—but definitely *not* human."

I nodded my thanks. I had seen enough.

"We're going to set up camp here tonight," I ordered the rest of the GASP members. "Find somewhere safe within the outer walls of the castle. Mona, Corrine, Ibrahim—get to work on the barriers. We should also take turns standing watch."

"I'll take the first few hours with Ben and Jeramiah," Lucas replied, glancing over at our sons.

I headed back up to Sofia and the rest of my family, looking around for a place to set up camp.

"At least it's vamp-friendly." Xavier gazed out beyond the walls of the castle with steel-gray eyes. "Not much else going for it."

"It will have to do until the dragons get back." I sighed. "Maybe they'll have come across something more suitable. I still feel like we're exposed out here, but it's better than nothing."

Rose shrugged. "I'm just glad to be in a place that's connected to the kids. At least we finally have proof that they're here…somewhere."

I nodded. *Somewhere.* I just prayed they were still alive.

Hazel

I watched as the ministers got to work creating barriers around the castle. The plan was that they would work in shifts—the ministers would maintain the force field around us night and day, protecting not only the castle but the multitude of villagers and guards who were camped within its grounds.

The Memenion castle was smaller than Hellswan, but much more welcoming. Everywhere I looked flowers and bushes grew, along with pretty trees—willows and apple—that made the whole place look more like an English manor house from a Jane Austen novel than the dark medieval vibe that Hellswan had encapsulated.

"The architecture here is *weird*," I commented to Ruby,

who was sitting on a fallen log, watching the comings and goings of the sentry army.

"I've noticed that." She grinned. "Especially as the last arrivals here were from the Viking era. Do you think they kept traveling through the portal and picking up styles from Earth?"

"I guess so. I can't figure out how else they would have come up with this." I looked back at the castle, seeing Tejus standing in the doorway. He beckoned us over and then disappeared back inside.

"We need to go." I nudged Ruby. "Come on."

Reluctantly, we made our way back toward the entrance. Both of us were too weary from the battle to want to do anything other than make small talk, completely avoiding the more important, life-threatening matters. The moment we'd arrived, I had tried to curl up on a sofa in the hallway, but I was too hyped to get rest—plus I'd dozed off on the back of Tejus's bull-horse for a while. I also knew there were decisions to be made—we couldn't stay here forever, afraid of the danger that we'd soon face. Those barriers wouldn't protect us from the entity, or its armies, whenever they decided to show up.

We met Ragnhild in the hallway, and Ruby flinched away. I knew her doubts about the lieutenant, but I thought Ruby should talk to him about it rather than constantly suspecting him. He had done nothing further to warrant our suspicion. I'd seen him fighting the Acolytes down at the cove—he certainly hadn't held back.

"The emperor and the commander are in the main banquet room. They're waiting for you," he announced stiffly, then gestured for us to follow him. Ruby—as the only one of us who had been here before—strode confidently in the right direction, overtaking the lieutenant.

We walked through marble arches and into the room, seeing Ash, Tejus and Queen Memenion already seated at a large table. Ragnhild left, disappearing back the way we'd just come. Ruby and I paused, unsure of the protocol, but Ash turned to us with an encouraging smile. We seated ourselves quietly. The mood was somber, and Queen Memenion kept her gaze fixed on the wooden table, her delicate features etched with misery. I imagined it was hard for her, being here without her family. I couldn't imagine what it was like for her, to lose her husband and son in the space of a few days.

"We need to decide what we're going to do next," Ash started, looking at each of us. "Tejus and I have decided to keep Jenus here as a prisoner, and hopefully he will give us some idea as to what the entity has in mind."

"What?" I burst out, shocked at the decision. It seemed unnecessarily dangerous to keep one of the entity's allies locked up with us—hadn't *anyone* learned lessons from what had happened with Queen Trina?

"We can't just let him fall into the hands of the entity—we are assuming he's able to communicate with it, and it's imperative that we get some answers." Tejus cut in. "Though we can't just wait around for my brother to divulge what he might know—it will take a while to break him down. In the meantime, we also need to find out what's happening at the cove. If that's where the entity is raising his army, then we need to be watching the area, finding out what we can about the enemy."

I sat back in my chair, chewing on my bottom lip while I considered how risky both moves would be. First, Jenus was nothing but a liability, and I didn't trust him as far as I could throw him. Second, we had fled the cove for good reason. Going back would be putting lives at risk. Still, if we could get to the portal…

"I think our best chance of surviving this is getting GASP involved," I announced. "We have jinn in The Shade. If a jinni locked up the entity in the first place, then they can do it again—the only problem is getting to the portal."

"I agree with Hazel," Ruby interjected. "We don't have a chance without the jinn—or the combined forces of GASP."

"It still leaves us with the same problem." Ash sighed. "I don't think we can send the army back there, not without knowing what kind of threat we're facing."

"Then we send a small group—reconnaissance only," Tejus argued. "While the rest of the army remain here, continuing to maintain the barriers. If the coast is clear, or there's a way to get through the portal unseen, then we retrieve GASP from Earth's dimension."

"Wait a moment." Queen Memenion looked confused. "I have absolutely no idea what you're talking about...what's GASP?"

Ruby and I filled the queen in on the nature of the inhabitants of The Shade. Her eyes widened as we detailed the supernatural creatures we had as friends, family and allies. She eyed Ruby and me more closely, stunned that we were the offspring of creatures she evidently hadn't thought existed. While she studied us, I felt her energy sort of 'brush up' against my own. Instantly a wave of hunger washed over me. I sat back further in my chair, catching Tejus's eye.

I need to feed, I spoke through our mental connection, hoping he would hear me.

He nodded, then turned his attention to Ash.

"I suggest Ragnhild and I go—maybe some other guards too."

Ash shook his head. "Tejus, you're too valuable. Send Ragnhild and some guards—the fewer the better. If it's just a reconnaissance mission, then they don't need you."

Tejus looked like he wanted to argue, but his eyes flickered over toward me, as if sensing the desperate need of my hunger.

"Fine," he snapped curtly. "The plan is set."

He stood up from his chair, the legs squeaking back across the marble floor.

"Hazel and I are going to visit my brother," he announced. Ash nodded in understanding, and the two of us left the room.

"This way." Tejus directed me swiftly along a corridor, and then off into a small, badly lit room. In the surface of the stone floor was a wooden hatch, a large barrel drawn over it.

"Where are the guards?" I asked. If this was Jenus's cell, then the place should have been flooded with heavily armed sentries.

"Down below—we're not taking any chances."

I nodded in relief as he removed the barrel and lifted up the hatch. A small stone staircase led into the gloom beneath. Maybe this castle was more medieval than I'd originally thought.

As I descended the steps after Tejus, guards started muttering to one another after they greeted him. When I reached the bottom, six of them surrounded a steel-barred cage in the center of the basement. Inside was the sniveling figure of Jenus. The guards bowed their heads in my direction – some of them even dropping forward on one knee. I looked at Tejus in confusion. He smiled, but didn't say anything.

Was this something to do with Queen Trina?

I frowned. It seemed strange, and kind of repulsive, that I would be respected for ending someone's life.

"I see you've brought the queen-killer to my door…is she hungry?" Jenus's voice cut across the gloom of the windowless space. "Not that I mind, of course," he continued in a wheedling voice. "I am more than happy to feed your monster, Tejus, if it means I am graced with this castle's protection."

"Silence," Tejus snapped. "Say another word and I'll have you meet the same fate as the rest of your mindless cult."

Jenus grimaced. "I don't know what you're talking about! I had *nothing* to do with them – nothing!"

"Go on." Tejus brushed my arm softly. "Take what you need."

I looked over at the guards. It made me uncomfortable to have them watching. Tejus picked up on my awkwardness, and turned to one of them.

"Can you give us a moment?" he asked. "If you would just wait above."

"Of course, Commander," the guard replied. He bowed his head again in my direction, his eyes meeting mine for a brief moment. They were clear and unwavering—and I couldn't avoid seeing the respect and awe in his glance. I smiled tentatively back, not knowing what else to do.

The guards left swiftly, leaving us alone with the captive.

"They love you, you know," Jenus cooed, breaking his silence. "Whoever would have thought that a mere scrap like you could bring down the mighty Queen Trina Seraq?"

Tejus kicked the bar with his foot.

"What the *hell* did I just say?" he hissed at his brother. "I am not making false threats, Jenus—your life is just about worthless right now, so don't tempt me."

I looked at Jenus in disgust. I almost loathed him more than I had Queen Trina—she might have been pure evil, but at least she had a spine. Then I remembered that he was providing dinner, so instead I smiled at him, and began to feed.

The energy flooded through me—it was dark and potent, so unlike the energy of Tejus or Ruby. It left a bitter taste in my mouth, and I immediately felt like I wanted a hot shower, but it was still energy, and I needed it. I drained Jenus till he was writhing around on the floor in pain. His agony should have made me pause, like it had done the day we'd rescued him from the forest prison, just before Tejus told me to stop, but this time I couldn't help myself. He deserved everything he got. The more I drank, the more the darkness of his energy became as tempting as it was repulsive.

I started to 'feel' around for memories – as unpracticed as I was, there were clear images that sifted like sand through Jenus's mind. I saw a pool of black tar, thick and gooey,

Queen Trina reclining back in it like she was taking a luxurious bubble-bath. The image was disturbing. I could also sense Jenus's lust for her in that moment and it made my own stomach heave.

"Enough," Tejus muttered.

Thank God.

I nodded, gently extricating my mind from Jenus's.

"You're a vile creature," he sniveled on the floor. "Foul like your lover! No different from the queen you killed in cold blood—no different from a common murderer!"

I rolled my eyes at Tejus. I'd heard enough of Jenus and his whining. Whatever dark energy I'd just taken from Jenus made me feel powerful and strong—no longer haunted by the small shreds of guilt at ending Queen Trina's life, no longer feeling an ounce of pity for my meal.

"Let's go," Tejus announced, holding out his hand. I took it gratefully, loving the feel of his skin against mine. I felt lust twisting and turning in my stomach, just as overwhelming as my hunger had been a few moments ago. Tejus smiled down at me, his eyes alight. I guessed he sensed what I was feeling.

We met the guards again at the top of the stairs, and they traipsed back down to maintain their watch. When we were back out in the light of the main corridor, Tejus turned to me.

"Hazel, you need to be careful—I should have thought

about this before, but taking...*dark* energy, like I sense Jenus's is right now, can have an effect." Tejus spoke softly, his arms snaking around my waist and pulling me toward him.

"I know," I replied honestly, looking up at him. "I can feel it. Maybe I should go easy on him, maybe use some of the other sentries like before—as long as they don't mind?" I asked, referring to the time that I'd syphoned off the accommodating minister by the walls of Hellswan.

"I think that would be a good idea."

"I also saw something... a memory, while I was syphoning. It was him and Queen Trina, sitting in some pool of tar-like liquid. It was powerful, whatever it was...and disturbing. I think you need to do the same. Maybe you can get more out of him than I can?" I hoped so. I didn't want to have to delve into Jenus's mind again. It was sick and twisted, but on the other hand, I didn't really like the thought of Tejus doing it either.

"Perhaps we were right then," he mused. "It sounds like – predictably – Jenus may have been drawn to whatever power was feeding Queen Trina. I'll take another look."

"You're dark enough already." I laughed. "It's a lot less dangerous for me to do it."

"We can argue about this later," he said, bringing his lips down to meet mine. The warmth of his lips sent shivers running up and down my spine.

"Do we have a room, or are we camping?" I asked softly, breaking away. His pupils were dilated, making his eyes almost completely black as he looked down at me.

"We have a room. You don't think I'd let my future wife sleep on the floor, do you?"

I felt heat rising to my cheeks at his words.

My future wife.

The idea made my head spin.

ROSE

The sunset was fading from the distance, casting even more darkness over the strange land. Now the gray piles of stones looked like hunched bodies, and we could see more clearly the small trickles of flame that were still burning down in the lower levels of the castle.

"I just can't bear waiting here like this. If we know the children aren't here, what are we waiting for?" Claudia's high-pitched tone came from the other side of the rubble pile I was perched on.

"I think it's better to be cautious," a softer, more musical voice replied. Claudia had obviously taken Sherus's sister, Lidera, hostage.

"In this instance, I don't," Claudia replied stoutly. "The moment I get my hands on Ruby's kidnappers I'm going to tear them limb from limb—rip the skin from their faces—"

"*Claudia.*"

I interrupted before the hot-headed vamp could traumatize the fae any further. I jumped swiftly over the pile, landing a few feet from Claudia. Her expression was furious.

"Don't tell me that you don't want to do the same, Rose— I'm just telling it like it is. We're all thinking the same thing."

"I know that, but maybe keep a lid on it until we find them? You're just going to make everyone more anxious than they already are," I argued.

"Try thinking about the bigger picture. It's not just your children who are in danger here," added Lidera, unhelpfully. Claudia hissed at her, and I groaned inwardly. I needed to keep Claudia occupied or we'd never get any peace. In the distance, I could see Yuri walking with Erik, overturning rubble in the hunt for clues as to what creatures might inhabit this dimension.

"Claudia, why don't you help Yuri? It will take your mind off things," I suggested.

"I'm going to find Ben," Lidera said, before Claudia could reply. As the copper-haired fae walked off, Claudia grunted in disapproval.

"I can't get used to the fae." She grimaced.

"But you're used to Ben, Lucas, and Grace?"

"They've only got the bodies of fae, not the weird mindset. The fae are so mysterious all the time, and...*hoity*. Like they think they're better than we are." Claudia continued her grumbling, but I blocked it out, trying to slowly edge the blonde vampire toward her husband. I knew why Claudia was being this way—she was just worried about the kids, and desperate to be doing something...but she was getting on my nerves.

As I herded her over to Yuri, I paused for a moment, standing frozen on a large piece of gray stone. I heard the unmistakable sound of wings flapping through the still night. The dragons were back.

Please have seen the kids.

"They're back!" I exclaimed, hurrying off in the direction of my father, with Claudia hot on my heels. I could see Grace and Lawrence running from another direction, followed by Aiden and then Caleb, and soon the whole team was gathered east of the palace, waiting impatiently for the dragons to land.

Lethe was the first to land, followed by Azaiah, Ridan and Jeriad.

"The army you heard leaving the cove is staying east from here, at another castle, this one unaffected by the earthquakes." Jeriad addressed his report to my father, while the others remained silent behind him. "Their numbers are significant—

some are camping outside. We can also see a strange barrier…almost like a translucent bubble covering the castle. We wouldn't have seen it except the sunset flared up at the right moment, revealing it. It's obviously some kind of magic."

Mona, Corrine and Ibrahim exchanged glances, looking concerned. I had never heard of a barrier that fit that description…but perhaps they had?

"The creatures are human-appearing in many respects, except they are freakishly tall. They ride strange horses that have the appearance of bulls, as well as using the vultures we thought we saw earlier for transport. We couldn't find out much more than that—the castle was heavily guarded."

"And the children?" my father asked.

Lethe shook his head, his eyes downcast. "We did not see them."

My head swam a bit as the disappointment floored me. Rationally, I had known that it was unlikely the dragons would return with news of the children, but that hadn't stopped me from holding onto a small sliver of hope.

"But they're still our best bet in locating the kids." Jeriad turned to me, his voice solemn. "We didn't see another soul as we flew over the land. I'm convinced that if the kids are anywhere, they're in that castle—perhaps under guard."

I nodded. At least we had a starting point.

"Thank you," I whispered.

"Let's get moving then," Claudia interjected.

My father glared at her. "Hold on. We *will* go to the castle, but I want to discuss the stones first. If this army has put some form of barrier up to protect themselves, then they're as threatened as we are by what those stones might contain."

I hadn't thought about that. Clearly we had the same enemy. I could only see it as good news; if we had the same goal in mind, then perhaps they would be up for negotiations.

"Nuriya," my father continued, addressing the jinni queen, "do you think you could close the stones at all – even if it's just temporarily keeping them sealed? Only for a short while to get us access to the portal?"

The jinni shook her head sadly. "That magic was lost to my people a long time ago. I traveled to see some of the elder jinn before we left, but none of them knew the magic of the stones—what was in them, or how to open them…so I am assuming none know how to close them either."

"What are you thinking?" my mother asked. "Why would we want to get back to the portal?"

Everyone turned to my father in confusion. We hadn't even come close to finding the children yet. Was he planning to leave already?

"I'm hoping that we can offer the army safe passage out of here—perhaps in return for the children, if they're keeping them hostage," my father replied. "And if not through the portal, perhaps some other land across the sea – wherever they might feel safe."

"Good idea." Ben nodded, catching on to his plan.

"But perhaps impossible," Sherus intoned, shaking his head. Clearly, he still thought arriving in this land had been a mistake. I was starting to feel a little impatient with the fae king—we were trying to save the In-Between too, it wasn't just our mission that we were here for.

"Are there any other ways in which we might be able to contain the stones?" my father asked again, looking at the witches.

"If we knew what was coming out of them, maybe," Ibrahim replied. "But if we don't know what we're up against…"

Suddenly, I had an idea. "Wait, surely if there are stones here, then the jinn that locked up these creatures can't be far away? Perhaps there's another group of jinn living in this dimension? Nuriya, is that possible?"

She shrugged, her jet-black hair bouncing in the moonlight. "It's possible, but if this land is as hostile as it seems, they would have wanted to leave – as your father says, perhaps somewhere across the ocean like The Dunes… assuming this really is the supernatural dimension. But still, there might be a chance they've remained here. I can't sense any, but that doesn't mean they're not around. Jinn are good at concealing themselves if necessary."

"But if there were jinn here, don't you think they'd be trying to close the stones already?" my mom asked. "It seems like a bit of a long shot."

"But perhaps the only chance we have," my father observed.

"And if there are jinn here, then the best way to find out would be getting to the castle…so let's get going." It was Claudia, riling my father yet again.

He sighed. "All right. We move out in an hour. Everyone get your packs ready. Leave whatever's not necessary, we need to travel light."

I nodded, hearing the unspoken implication that if anything went wrong we might have to run for our lives.

The group dispersed, and I was left standing with Caleb.

"Are you okay?" he asked, lifting my chin up to meet his gaze.

"Tired, worried, anxious…the list kind of goes on… You?"

"The same. I'm glad Claudia's pushing your father to get to the castle. It's the not knowing that's driving me crazy."

I nodded. "I get why he's being cautious—if Sherus is right then this enemy's going to be unlike anything we've faced before…but all I can think about is Hazel and Benedict. Were they in this castle when it came crashing down?" I shivered. They left here alive, according to the werewolves, but that didn't mean they hadn't been wounded or afraid.

"Let's try not to think about it," Caleb replied softly.

"I know, but I can't help it."

"We have to keep believing that they're fine, Rose, or we won't make it through this."

My husband was right. I grasped his hand in mine, squeezing it gratefully. We were getting closer all the time. I shouldn't be giving up hope now.

Julian

"All I can think about is how we're being left out, *again*," Benedict huffed, trying to get comfortable on the stone floor. "I think we would be good on a recon mission—we're smaller than the sentries, so we could get closer without being seen. Which I *would* have pointed out *if* we'd been invited."

We'd listened in secretly to the meeting that Ash and Tejus had held, knowing that they'd be making plans for our next attack. Now we'd found a corner of the castle where we could remain undisturbed. I had just wanted to get away from the craziness of the close-to-bursting castle, but Benedict saw it as an opportunity to plot our way into the action.

"Do you really think that's a good idea?" I asked. "I mean—

all those stones opening? We don't even know what's in them...and the entity? Not sure I want to come face to face with that." I felt queasy at the thought. I didn't understand how Benedict was so up for reuniting with the power that had possessed him. Maybe he'd conveniently forgotten how scared he'd been? How scared we'd *all* been? From the days of our short-lived Hell Raker group, I'd definitely had a change of heart about blindly going off to battle the beasts and evils that Nevertide had lurking in every corner. I'd learnt my lesson after a stint in Queen Trina's dungeons. Clearly Benedict still hadn't.

"It's just a recon mission, Julian. We won't actually have to fight them or anything. I want to know what's going to come out of those stones."

"Well, I don't think we can." I sighed. "We can't get out of here—the barriers are going to be heavily guarded and watched the whole time. And if you think Hazel and Ruby will let us go, then you've gone mad."

Benedict tugged on a leaf of the nearest potted plant, his face gloomy.

"This sucks," he moaned.

"Do you want to go and look at the fang-beasts?" I asked, trying to cheer him up. The bizarre creatures that Queen Memenion had begun keeping as pets had been penned up near the stables. They looked like wolves, but much larger and about a million times more ferocious. Like testosterone-injected wolves with rabies.

"Why don't we hide in the stables? That way, when Ragnhild and the rest of them ride out, we can hide beneath the bull-horses or something and run out with them?" Benedict's eyes lit up.

"That's so *stupid*."

Yelena echoed my thoughts perfectly. She strode around the corner of the wall we'd been leaning against, hands on her hips, looking down pityingly at us both.

"What are you doing here?" Benedict groaned. "I thought you were with the others—and by the way, that's not a very polite way to speak to the person who saved your *life*. Twice!"

She rolled her eyes. "I already said thank you—what else do you want, a medal?"

"Wouldn't mind."

I exhaled in frustration. I'd thought that Benedict and Yelena would get along better now that Benedict had put his neck out for her in such heroic ways, but clearly not. I was starting to think that they actually enjoyed aggravating one another.

"I actually have a better plan," Yelena announced.

"Surprise, surprise," Benedict muttered.

She cast him a baleful look before continuing.

"I've done a bit of investigating of my own, and there are a couple of places where the barrier isn't guarded as well as it should be. I think, if you want to join the recon mission, we take a horse *now* and hide out behind the stables…there's loads of wild, overgrown bushes and trees near there. When the army leaves in the morning, we wait till the last moment, before the barrier closes, and ride right out! Getting far away enough that they can't send us back!"

This still sounded highly dubious to me.

"That was *my* plan!" Benedict exclaimed. "You've literally just said my plan back to me!"

"It's completely different," Yelena corrected, "and doesn't have the stupid idea of hiding beneath a horse. Seriously, that would never work."

I let them argue on while I thought about the logistics of it. And how much trouble we'd be in when we got found out.

"I don't think this is a good idea," I interrupted.

"Why not?" Yelena asked.

"For one, it's dangerous, and two, Ragnhild will most definitely send us back when he finds us. We'll probably end up chained next to Jenus for the rest of our lives."

Yelena pulled a face. "Julian, come on—we need to know what we're up against. Perhaps we'll recognize the creatures that came out of the sea better than the sentries—they didn't even know what a jingi was, remember?"

"*Jinni*," Benedict corrected, "and neither do you."

They had a point. The sentries didn't seem to have much of a grasp on the supernatural world, which was weird considering the ghouls, goblins and nymphs roaming about the place.

"This has disaster written all over it," I pointed out.

"We've been in danger since we got here. I don't see how this is going to make any difference—and it might help us." Benedict wasn't going to be swayed.

"I swear you have the worst short-term memory of anyone I've ever met," I grumbled. No doubt as soon as we got near the cove, Benedict would once again be terrified half to death, and wish he'd never suggested this crazy-ass plan.

"Let's at least go to the stables and see if it's possible?" Yelena pleaded.

"Fine." I sighed reluctantly. "But if we can't get out without being seen then we're not going—agreed?"

"Agreed," they both chorused, their tones sullen. I felt like a babysitter in charge of the most reckless kids alive. *Lucky me.*

Hazel

The room we'd been given was opulent, full of fabrics designed to add some comfort to the austere marble of the floor and walls. In the middle of the room there was a large four-poster bed, covered in cream sheets and throws interlaced with gold thread. It looked like an incredibly lavish hotel room, the kind that a couple might stay in during a honeymoon. The only difference was the bars on the window—thick iron poles that had obviously been added recently, as they clashed with the rest of the castle's interior. It was a blunt reminder that we were at war, and we didn't know what tomorrow would bring.

Tejus was in the en-suite bathroom, and I could hear the cascading of water as he showered. I had already bathed, and had started pacing up and down the room anxiously. My lower stomach knotted, and light butterfly flickers of anticipation danced inside of me every time I looked at the bed. We were supposed to be getting rest while we could — waiting for the dawn to rise, and then the moment that Ragnhild would return from the cove, letting us know what we were up against. I didn't feel like resting though. My mind felt like it was scattered in a million different directions.

I pulled at my top and grimaced at my pants, wishing that I had some clothes that Tejus hadn't seen me wear a hundred times already. I had the feeling that tonight would be special. I *wanted* it to be special...But there was a darker thought nudging at the edge of my consciousness, one that wasn't so welcome. Without wanting to look too deeply into it, I felt a sense of finality pervading everything. Maybe it was because the air was so still, or that this was the pause before the storm began. I didn't really know. I just had an inescapable feeling that tonight was the end of something.

The door to the bathroom opened. Tejus stood in the doorway with a towel wrapped around his waist, his hair wet and slicked back with droplets still running off his neck and down his chest. I could see the scars from the ghoul's claws across his chest, and the symbol that had been carved on his pectoral—still slightly pink round the edges where it hadn't finished healing.

I can't believe this man wants to marry me.

The thought went around and around in my head as I stared at him, the butterflies becoming more intense and my heart palpitating in my chest. I suddenly felt like I wasn't worthy—whatever I had to offer him just didn't seem *enough*. Without realizing what I was doing I wrapped my arms around my torso. I realized too late that it wasn't exactly welcoming body language.

Tejus frowned slightly.

"Hazel?"

"I'm fine," I replied, my voice catching in my throat.

He looked like he wanted to say something, but changed his mind at the last moment. Instead he cleared his throat, and gestured at the floor.

"I'll make a bed here," he reassured me gently.

"No, wait. I think I can handle it… with the hunger, I mean," I replied, feeling heat blast across my cheeks. He was silent for a few moments, eyeing me speculatively.

"Can you come here, please?" he asked eventually. "I'd come to you, but it looks like you're going to run out of the door if I make any sudden movements."

"I'm nervous," I replied, shutting my eyes briefly as I felt embarrassment consume me.

"I can tell. But I don't understand why."

His tone was warm, without a hint of accusation—it went a

little way in helping me calm my erratic heartbeat.

"I don't really know," I whispered. "I guess last time…it was all in the heat of the moment, and now…I don't know, I just feel so awkward."

"Hmm," he murmured, a small smile lifting at the corners of his mouth. "Making people feel at ease isn't exactly my strong point."

I grinned. "You're right about that."

"But I'm going to try."

I eyed him skeptically, but his expression was solemn—he wasn't joking.

"Okay then," I mumbled.

He walked toward me, and I tilted my head upward as he approached, expecting him to kiss me. Instead he smiled softly, and lowered his lips to my ear.

"Turn around," he whispered.

Unable to speak, I nodded, slowly turning as he'd commanded. I faced the fire at the end of the room, staring into the bright yellow flames. I could feel Tejus's breath tickling the base of my neck, sending shivers multiplying across my skin. I felt his hands running through my hair, clasping the strands together and moving them over one of my shoulders. A soft kiss was planted on the back of my neck—so soft it could have just been my imagination. I stopped breathing.

"When I was younger, one of the stable workers told me that

the best way to calm a skittish animal is to talk softly, to let them listen to your voice, until they trust you enough to eat out of your hand," Tejus murmured, his lips lightly pressed against the top of my head. He ran his thumb down my bare arm. I took a deep, steadying breath.

"You hate talking," I whispered.

"No," he breathed, "I just think it's overrated. But perhaps it's necessary now."

He remained standing behind me, but moved his hands around my waist, running his fingers along the band of my pants. All I could hear was the sound of our breathing and the soft scratch of his skin on the fabric of my clothing.

"The best way to keep talking is to recite things you've memorized," he continued.

"Like what?"

"Well"—his fingers came to rest on the curve of my hip—"things like you have a small beauty spot here, and another here." His fingers moved upward a fraction, over my jeans. "And one here. They make an almost perfect line."

I swallowed, my insides feeling like they had turned to mush.

"You have a birthmark here," he continued, running his hand down the front of my thigh, and round to the curvature of my backside.

"And down here." His hands continued to travel down my

leg, and his body moved to crouch on the ground. His hand stopped at my kneecap. "You have a small scar, just above this bone."

"How do you remember all that?" I whispered as he moved back up to stand behind me. I was fully dressed – there was no way he'd be seeing all this. If it was from memory, then he must have really studied my body the night we'd spent together in Hellswan…

"How could I not?"

I bit my lip, feeling his body move closer to mine. I leaned back against him, my fear and awkwardness slowly seeping away to be replaced with the need to be as close to Tejus as possible.

His hands moved down to the hem of my top.

"Shall we see if I was right?"

I smiled, lifting my arms upward. He removed the shirt, letting it drop to the floor. He ran slow kisses along my neck, unhooking my bra. Instead of lowering my arms, I reached backward and upward, wrapping my hands around his neck, feeling the dampness of his hair between my fingers.

His hands ran down the sides of my body, and I exhaled sharply at the tremors that shook me in response to his touch. He stepped back, removing my pants while I balanced myself by placing my hands on his shoulders.

"It worked." I smiled.

"Then will you come to bed with me?"

I nodded.

He stood, and then lifted me up into his arms in one swift movement, carrying me over to the bed. He didn't let go of me until we were both beneath the covers, our legs entwined.

The moonlight shone through the bars of the window, creating ever-shifting lines across our bodies. Our lips met, our kisses instantly deep, each one causing me to surrender my breath entirely. I arched toward him, not wanting an inch of space between us. His body felt so solid, so reassuring, anchoring me to our reality as every other part of my being seemed to melt away.

As we made love, I started to feel our minds melding together, my thoughts running into his and every exhale and breath of his seeming like it was my own. I could see myself through his eyes, startled by the vision of my hair fanned out across the pillow, my skin beading with perspiration as I moved to his rhythm—my eyes wide, pupils dilated in desire.

"Are you doing this?" I breathed in wonder.

"We're doing this."

I exhaled, my mind and body feeling like they were going to implode. I'd never known it was possible to feel this close to another living thing—as if where I ended he began, our nerve endings connected, every touch felt by us both and amplified so that when his lips grazed the curve of my shoulder, I felt it in the tips of my toes, on the base of my spine, in the blood that screamed through my veins.

His mind whispered through mine, the wisps of thought familiar and strange at the same time. I could hear his voice, flowing like water into me.

I love you…I love you…be mine.

It sounded like a prayer.

"Tejus," I responded out loud in a breath, looking up into the black pools of his eyes. "I… I love you. I'll always be yours."

It was only afterward, lying in Tejus's embrace, that I finally understood why I'd thought that tonight was the end of something.

It was. It was the end of an old life—one that I'd outgrown without realizing it. My human life. It was over; my body had known before I did, becoming stronger and more resilient as I transformed into a sentry, knowing desire, love and rage in quantities I'd never experienced as a human. Now my head was playing catch-up, and it had taken seeing myself through Tejus's eyes to finally realize what I had become.

I also knew, without a shadow of a doubt, that I was no longer alone. Wherever I was, whatever I was, part of my soul would always be searching for his.

BENEDICT

"I'm freezing," Yelena whined.

"This was *your* idea," I retorted. We had been waiting in the cold for hours, crouching low behind the back of the stables so that none of the ministers or guards would see us. There was a thorny bush digging into my back, and no matter how many times I shifted about I still couldn't get comfortable.

We had taken one grumpy bull-horse out of the stable and covered it in a blanket and our robes in order to keep him warm. So far it had been quiet—it had caused a bit of fuss when we tried to take it from its pen, but after we'd fed it hay and Yelena had insisted on brushing its coat, the creature had settled and then fallen asleep. Dawn was fast approaching and

I hoped that the guards would be here soon.

"Keep your voices down," Julian whispered. He had been irritable all night, and I worried that at any moment he was going to change his mind and go back to the castle. I hoped not—there was no way I was doing this without him. I kept expecting to hear Ruby or Hazel calling out to us from the castle, but they must have been busy with the kids or sleeping, because I hadn't seen them since we'd eavesdropped on the meeting.

I was starting to question the wisdom of this entire plan— at least if we'd done what I suggested we'd be warm in the stables, snuggled up against the bull-horses and hay bales. But Yelena always thought she knew better…which was probably why I spent so much of my time saving her ass.

"I think I hear something." Yelena rose up on her knees, listening. I did the same. A few moments later footsteps approached, and Ragnhild's voice cut across the yard.

"Get the bull-horses ready, the fastest we've got."

The door to the stables creaked open, and the bull-horses started to whinny in greeting. Now was our chance. We crept over to our bull-horse, who had woken up at the sound of his friends—I hoped that it wouldn't make a sound, and that its absence wasn't going to be noticed. Hopefully we'd taken one of the slower ones.

The guards proceeded to walk the bull-horses around the

stable yard, loading on saddles and weapons.

"You keep watch," Julian murmured to me, "Yelena and I will get the horse ready."

I nodded in agreement, peering as closely as I dared around the side of the stable. Soon, each of the guards had mounted a bull-horse and Ragnhild sat atop his, giving orders to the ministers on duty to open the barriers.

"We need to move now!" I hissed, running back to Julian and Yelena. Both of them were already sitting on its back, and Yelena reached out her arm to pull me up. I scrambled on— not a moment too soon. Hooves clattered as the army rode across the grounds, heading in the direction of the opening in the barrier.

"Go, go!" Julian spurred on the bull-horse with the reins.

Nothing happened. The bull-horse lowered its head, munching on the grass.

"Julian, do something!" I cried.

"I'm *trying*!"

"Do you think it only responds to sentries?" Yelena asked.

"No—I saw Ruby ride one," I spluttered. Maybe it just needed a bit more encouragement…Leaning back, I smacked the bull-horse on the rump as hard as I could. It reared up, and I held on fast to Yelena. The bull-horse shot out from behind the stables, following the rest of the army.

The guards were so intent on navigating their way through

the tents that covered the gardens of the palace that they didn't turn around at our approach. Julian managed to gain a bit more control over our ride, and soon we were passing through the barriers with the rest of Ragnhild's small army. A few ministers gave us puzzled looks, but they didn't say anything—I guessed for all they knew we might have been requested on the mission.

We clattered down the pathway that would eventually lead to the main road that ran through Nevertide. Thanks to the dim light of the dawn, and the fact that half the sky was still midnight black, none of the other riders seemed to notice us. We stayed a few paces back from the last three riders at the end of the line, just to be safe. As long as they remained unaware of our presence till we got near the cove, there would be no way that we'd be sent back—it would be too dangerous for us to travel through Nevertide alone.

As we approached the main road, I held my breath. The turn was sharp enough for Ragnhild to see us if he looked sideways. Luckily, he navigated the bend head-on, continuing to ride at a fast pace without closely observing his troops.

We didn't say a word to one another as the journey progressed. The dawn rose fully, and I started to feel a bit warmer—especially as I had to tense every muscle in my body just to stay on the horse. Ragnhild never let up his speed, and neither did any of the other riders.

Suddenly, just before the turn that would take us to the

cove, the line came to an abrupt halt. Julian didn't stop the bull-horse in time, and so it reared up with a loud neigh, nearly ramming into the butt of one of its friends.

"Order!" Ragnhild yelled, riding down the line to see what the disturbance was.

Oh, crap.

"What are you doing here?" he thundered, catching sight of the three of us.

"We thought we'd join you," I replied, as confidently as I could. Maybe if it seemed like no big deal, he'd just accept it?

"WHAT?"

Okay. Maybe not.

"Look," Julian replied, using his reasonable, grown-up tone that made him sound like a news presenter, "we just thought that we might be able to help—the entity's army might be made up of supernatural creatures that we're familiar with."

"Does the emperor know you're here?" Ragnhild raged, completely ignoring Julian's argument.

"No," I replied, "but I'm sure Ash will be glad when he finds out—glad that we wanted to help."

Ragnhild glared at me, and I half-thought he was going to punch me.

"Do you know how much trouble you're going to be in when you get back? How much trouble *I'm* going to be in?"

"Not if we succeed," I pointed out.

"You're kids!" he cried. "This is madness! Tergor, take them back to the castle. I can't waste any more time with this."

One of the guards grunted, and pulling up next to us, he grabbed the reins from Julian.

"Just let us come!" I cried out, realizing that I'd underestimated how pissed off Ragnhild would be. "Tejus said that this was a recon mission only, and we're smaller than you, so we'll have a better chance of escaping unseen. Please," I begged. "I was the one under the entity's influence—at least let me help bring it down!"

Tergor the guard grinned, turning back to Ragnhild with a questioning look on his face. Clearly the guard didn't like the idea of heading back to the castle any more than we did.

"This is madness," Ragnhild muttered again, his jaw clenched. He wasn't yelling anymore though, which, if I compared it to experiences with my parents, was usually a sign that we were winning.

"We'll stay back from the shore—we'll just watch from the cove," I added, not meaning it—but he didn't need to know that.

Ragnhild looked in the direction of the ocean. The sky was getting steadily lighter—we were running out of time.

"You stay back," he hissed, "and when we return to the castle, I want your word that you'll tell Ashbik the truth—that this was all *your* idea."

"Agreed!" piped up Yelena brightly.

Jeez. Of all the times for the bossiest person in the world to stay silent.

"Didn't fancy arguing our cause?" I muttered in her ear as we continued to ride.

"You were doing perfectly well on your own. I didn't want to remind him that he had a helpless human girl on his mission," she replied smugly.

Helpless? Hardly.

"Will you two be quiet?" Julian snapped.

I shut my mouth, realizing that I was pushing my friend to breaking point.

We carried on riding alongside Tergor, now moving at a slower pace as we approached the cove. I glanced over at the guard a couple of times, but he didn't speak to us. Beads of sweat formed on his temples, and his ruddy face grew paler as we continued our journey. He was scared, I could see it.

Why aren't I?

I held onto Yelena with a steady grip, my breathing regular, my skin without sweat or goosebumps. We were traveling to the cove, the place where I'd almost lost my mind with fear time and time again. Where I'd been possessed, taken hostage by forces so dark and evil that I could barely believe they existed. I wondered if I was done with fear—my body, and my mind just couldn't fit any more in. Somehow I'd become immune.

"Are you afraid?" I asked Yelena, thinking that it might not just be me.

"Why?" she snapped, affronted.

"I just want to know—honestly. Are you?"

"I've been afraid since the day I got here. Doesn't mean I have to turn and run away from it."

Her reply surprised me. I had thought that Yelena was so bossy and bull-headed that maybe all of Nevertide's horrors had just passed her by, that she'd taken it all on the chin. It reminded me of something my dad had said—that true courage was when you accepted your fears, but did whatever you were afraid of anyway. I guessed Yelena was just courageous. Maybe—though I didn't want to admit it—she was just a little braver than I had ever been. Obviously, I would never actually *tell* her that.

Ragnhild signaled for the troop to stop. We all came to a halt, Julian struggling slightly with the bull-horse, until Tergor leant over and gave a hard yank on its reins. We all began to dismount—we would be traveling the rest of the way on foot.

"You and you"—Ragnhild pointed at two of the guards—"check that the coast is clear up on the cliff. If it's safe, the rest of us will travel down the passage."

The guards nodded, and hurried off.

"The rest of you, wait here until I say so." The lieutenant

glared directly at the three of us. I nodded meekly, not in any hurry to defy him again.

"Ashbik is going to demote me," he muttered. "Then Tejus is going to lynch me."

As I glanced over at the lieutenant, a thought occurred to me.

"Is that why you came down to the cove, telling Ruby that Ash had sent you to keep her safe?"

The lieutenant glowered.

"How do you know about that?" he shot back.

"Ruby told us." I rolled my eyes. "Everyone thought you might be an Acolyte."

"*What?*" he asked. "I only went along because I thought if I saved Ruby or Hazel it would guarantee my position—I've wanted to be lieutenant of the Hellswan army for as long as I could remember."

Julian shook his head, clearly thinking along the same lines as me—Ragnhild had nearly got himself banished, never mind demoted.

"Maybe just tell the truth in the future," I muttered.

Ragnhild looked like he was going to chastise me, but at that moment, the two guards appeared back from the cliff. They looked more puzzled than frightened—maybe nothing had happened?

"There's definitely something down there," one of the

guards explained breathlessly, "but you'll have to see it for yourself…I can't see any obvious danger—though the sea, it's still frozen." He shook his head, disbelieving. "I've never seen anything like it."

"All right." Ragnhild nodded his thanks. "We travel down to the cove. Is everyone ready? Weapons to hand. You three"—he looked down at us with thinly veiled distaste—"you go last. And if I tell you to get out of there, you do what I say, understood?"

"Understood," Julian replied firmly.

"Then let's head out."

Ragnhild led the procession, following the rocky path down to meet the shore. I could see the extent of the earthquake's devastation—though it had left the actual cove alone, the cliff had collapsed in some parts, and the passage, carved over time into the rock, had become much more narrow. We followed him in single file, Julian leading the three of us. Yelena reached back and grabbed my hand in hers, squeezing too tightly.

Footsteps were made as quietly as we possibly could, with only the occasional snap of a dried twig or the slight slide of loose gravel.

Soon Ragnhild had passed through the passage, and we followed him out onto the curve of the cove.

"I can't *see* anything." I nudged Julian for him to move out of the way as Yelena dipped back behind me.

Julian didn't answer me. His eyes were fixed ahead. At first I thought he was looking at the frozen ocean—the tidal wave suspended in mid-air, looking as if it would crash down and drown us at any moment. Without waiting for him to move, I pushed my way past him—and stopped.

Where the Acolytes had been chanting on the shore, there was now a *thing*. A black heap a few feet high. Out of the top a dome rose—it was made up of the same semi-translucent material as the barriers the sentries made, but inside it, sparks of electricity ricocheted off the surfaces like lightning. It looked like there was a storm inside the dome, and in the center, one thick rope of energy—blindingly bright, all the colors of the rainbow shooting through it.

"What the hell is that?" I breathed.

"I have no idea," Ragnhild replied, glancing down at me with an unreadable expression. "Nothing good."

"It looks like a...conductor or something," I whispered. "But where's the energy coming from?"

"The bodies."

Ragnhild looked back at the dome. I was confused—*what bodies*? I crept closer, squinting against the light of the dome. Oh. The black heap. It was made up of the bodies of the fallen Acolytes...maybe even Queen Trina too, though I couldn't make out any individual figures. But the dome suddenly made sense—the 'lightning' was being sucked from the dead, and pouring into the larger conductor in the middle...but where was it going? Down into the earth?

Ragnhild's hand landed heavily on my shoulder, making me jump.

"No further, Benedict."

I stood still.

"We'll go around the edge. I want to get a closer look at the stones," Ragnhild continued in a low tone.

I nodded, following the rest of the guards and Julian as we quietly crept around the edges of the cliff, heading toward the sea. As we passed the dome, I could see that the dead Acolytes had been piled up in an almost perfect circle...who had done that?

As we neared the frozen sea, I started to feel uneasy.

There's something here.

It wasn't the dome, but something else, coming from the sea. I couldn't even begin to describe it, or really understand why I was feeling the way I was—I just knew that there was something, *something*, waiting for us by the water.

"Ragnhild," I hissed, "I don't think we should go any further."

He looked back at me, his face a ghostly white. He could feel it too. I turned to Julian. His expression was tortured, like he had just come face to face with some unspeakable fear. It was the stuff of nightmares, like when you thought there was something looking out at you from the closet in the middle of the night, and though you couldn't see anything, you knew it was there—waiting, watching you in the dark.

"We need to go back," I whispered urgently. "We need to *go*."

I took a step back, and my foot crunched on something. Looking down, I saw one of the stones. It must have rolled out from the sea bed. I bent down to get a closer look. It had broken in half like an eggshell. I thought maybe I had done that, but when I looked toward the sea bed, none of them remained whole any more. They had all opened up.

"The stones…th-th-they've opened," Ragnhild stuttered, coming to the same realization as I had.

The air seemed to stir, as if we'd woken something…

"Now—we leave now! It's coming – something's coming!" I called out to Ragnhild, no longer worried that my voice was too loud. I didn't care about anything apart from getting as far away from this place as possible.

I yanked Yelena's arm. She hadn't moved since we'd come close to the sea bed. I would drag her away from here if I needed to. We all started to run. Blood pounded in my head, blocking my eardrums to any other sound than the beating of my heart. I screamed as I felt a jolt from behind me, but it was just a guard picking me up—running with me and Yelena in each arm, back to the passage.

JENUS

He had awoken.

Something had happened, finally. I had been afraid that Queen Trina and the Acolytes had not been successful—that they had met their end before their task was done. The land had been so silent, the guards and sentries almost jubilant, as if they had conquered what evil there was in Nevertide.

Fools.

In the darkness of my cell I could hear him whispering to me once again. The promises he had once made to Queen Trina were now offered to his most loyal servant—still alive, still dedicated to his ultimate rise. Promises that would leave me blessed by all his power—to share in his glory, and his reign.

"What do you ask of me, benevolent lord?" I muttered in the darkness, over and over again, too low for the pot-bellied and mead-soaked guards who surrounded me to hear. They wouldn't understand my worship anyway. They worshiped nothing but themselves, and the false emperor, and my brother — a being even more wretched and broken than myself. I had been offered salvation in the form of the entity, a gift my brother would never receive.

Come to me, my son, the voice would whisper, *come to me, and taste a freedom you have never known.*

Images wound their way through my mind with the soft caress of a lover. Me, sitting on the imperial throne, staff in one hand, a decree of my rule in the other. On my head the crown, gold and opulent, finally placed on the scalp of its rightful owner. Women who looked like angels, dancing around me in attendance, their silks and gauze brushing up against my skin, their eyes pools of lust as they beheld me in all my power and greatness. And then my brother, the greatest prize of all, sniveling at my feet, begging for my mercy—clutching the ruined, blood-soaked body of his once-human love, her eyes glassy in death, staring up at the stars, her body cold and ready for the grave.

All this will be yours, Jenus of Hellswan, all this and more...

"What do I do?" I cried out, rattling the bars of my cage. I was trapped—tricked by Queen Trina in her last hours—left to the mercy of my brother and the rest of the armies of the six kingdoms. I supposed she'd thought they would end me when they saw me in the Seraq kingdom, the fool. She underestimated the mercy of men—Tejus's childish hope that one day I would love him again.

But what was I to do? The bars of my cage seemed unbreakable, and even with the roaring drunkenness of the guards who shared this dank hole with me, they watched me closely, their eyes never leaving me. They ensured that the barriers that surrounded me, along with the bars of my cage, never let up.

The only time they had left me, and the barriers had come down, was at Tejus's request, so his pet monster might feed off me. But even then, I was helpless—weakened by her greed. I couldn't fight Tejus, not in this decaying body. It had been so long since I'd entered the tar-like waters at Queen Trina's palace—so long since I'd felt the true force of my lord running freely within my veins. I didn't have the strength to stand up to Tejus. If I faltered, if he overpowered me, I would be killed. They would see through my lies, see how much I desired escape—if they didn't already.

"What do I do?" I called into the darkness, hopeless.

He did not answer me, the whispers had gone silent. Had I displeased him? But what choice did I have? There was no friend left to me—the Acolytes were dead, Queen Trina with them. Not that *she* was ever much of a friend. I alone was the sole worshiper of my lord, and now he was silent.

"Don't abandon me!" I called again—a whine, a plea.

"Will you stop that racket!" A guard kicked the cage, and like vermin, I shrank back. Would my lord leave me like this— barely able to fend off the insults and jabs from a group of third-class citizens, so beneath me, so beneath my unspoiled lineage?

I held my head in my hands, despair taking over, feeling the absence of my lord's benevolence and love like a deep wound in my heart.

ASH

"What now?"

Ruby was standing on the balcony that overlooked the rear gardens of the castle. She had been anxiously fiddling with the hem of her robe, pulling at the loose threads as she looked at the rows of tents that had taken over Queen Memenion's gardens.

"We wait," I replied simply.

There was nothing else we could do, other than maintain the strength of the barriers, until Ragnhild's team returned to the castle with news.

"The hardest part." She smiled ruefully.

"I know."

Tell me about it.

The wait, the build-up…it was hellish.

"Everything seems so peaceful…it's unnerving. Do you think there's a chance that this could all be over?" she asked, her blue eyes half-hopeful.

I shook my head. No way was this over—the book had promised armies rising from the sea, the entity rising to full power. I didn't believe for a second that the death of Queen Trina and the Acolytes would have put an end to any of it. This was too powerful, so much bigger than the lives of a few sentries.

"I think we need to be prepared for the worst," I said quietly. "But this is usual for you, right, with GASP and all the supernatural stuff you deal with?"

I'd been trying to get my head around Ruby's family and home for a while now. I was having a hard time imagining that such a place existed—that she had been exposed to so much strangeness all her life. I had just assumed that Ruby had come from an ordinary home, like me. To find out her life had been so extraordinary took some getting used to.

"I wasn't a fully-fledged member—not yet…" She paused, realizing that she was implying that one day she would leave here—go back home. We hadn't really discussed anything like that since I'd become emperor. Things were very different from when we'd first begun talking about Earth. I had imagined leaving Nevertide, entering another land as her boyfriend, getting used to things like television, s'mores, game consoles and everything else. Now I didn't know what the future held— whether or not I'd be permitted to leave, whether or not I'd want to leave my people behind if we survived this.

"Don't worry." I swallowed, trying to adopt an easy manner. "I know you'll want to go home when you can…I don't blame you. I thought working as a cook in Hellswan's kitchens was bad. This is something *else*."

She laughed. "Yeah. Things do seem to have gone from bad to worse pretty quickly. The kingship trials look like kids' play now, right?"

"The power of perspective." I grinned.

She turned back to the gardens, her smile dropping. Vultures were flying about inside the barrier, getting exercise. One hurtled across the length of the balcony, squawking loudly and making us both jump.

"I hope you choose to join me," she said once we'd both recovered.

"On Earth?"

"Yeah, in The Shade. You'd be an asset."

To you or to GASP? I wondered, hoping it was the former. I stayed silent, not sure how to respond…I didn't want to make any false promises to Ruby, and in my heart of hearts, I was hoping that once this was all over, she'd change her mind and want to stay here. I knew that Nevertide could be better—together we could change it, turn it into a place she'd be proud to rule by my side.

"Or at least visit on vacation?" she asked softly, her eyes downcast.

"I can't answer you yet, Shortie. All I know is that I never want us to be apart, and I'm trying to come up with a way that we can work around that."

She nodded, turning away from me again.

This is not going the way I planned.

I felt like I was messing this up, badly. I knew that these few moments of quiet were the only ones we'd get for a while; I had wanted us to do something special. I had wanted to remind her that we were good together—that although the odds felt stacked against us, we'd find a way to work things out. Because we had to. For me, there was no other option.

"Come on." I held out my hand. "Come somewhere with me."

She willingly placed her hand in mine, looking up at me expectantly. I grinned, trying to look like I had a plan in mind...because I had no idea where we were going. Somewhere more private than this, that was for sure. Anywhere that we couldn't see an entire sentry army would be good...

I pulled her gently back into the castle, heading for the towers. I was pretty sure I'd seen sentries at the watch posts when we'd arrived—maybe I could politely request some privacy…there had to be some plus points to being emperor.

"Where are we going?" She laughed.

"You'll see…"

"I didn't think you knew this castle?"

I don't.

"I know everything, Shortie. You should know that by now," I teased, hoping she bought my bluff.

The door to the tower was open, and I smiled broadly down at Ruby as we made our way up the stairs. After some effort—I hadn't expected the climb to be quite so high—we reached the top. A small wooden doorway led out to a narrow platform built around the tower. The only thing between us and a mile-long drop was a thin iron railing that only reached up to the top of my shoe, clearly for decorative purposes only.

"Um, you don't suffer from vertigo, do you?" I asked, feeling slightly queasy as I looked down.

"No…but this is slightly scary, Ash."

"But look around," I replied brightly, "the whole of Nevertide…"

This was a mistake.

"It's amazing," she conceded slowly. "But why have you brought me up here?"

"Well… I thought it might be nice. Romantic, maybe?"

She started to giggle, covering her mouth with her hand,

doing her best to hold it back.

"I'm so sorry," she gasped. "I don't mean to laugh…It's just… this is *terrifying*. I feel like I'm going to plummet to my death at any moment."

"I know," I groaned, half laughing, half disbelieving that I'd messed this up so badly. "I didn't really have time to plan this."

"Plan what, though?" she replied, trying to collect herself. "I don't understand. If you want to spend some time together, let's just go back to our room?"

The words were said with a shy smile, and I kicked myself. Why hadn't I just done that? We would have had privacy there. Why did I have to go and make this so complicated? Ruby turned back toward the door, beckoning me back down the stairs.

I wanted to follow, but I was fast losing my nerve. If I didn't say it now, I was afraid I'd never get the words out of my mouth.

"Ruby, wait," I called out.

She turned, looking at me expectantly.

"I have something I need to ask you. I know things are…*unsettled* between the two of us, but I wanted to say this now rather than later…just in case anything happens." I took a few moments, trying to breathe—to say the right words.

"Ash?" she questioned, her voice high-pitched and frightened. "What's going on? You're acting really weird, has something happened?"

I shook my head, realizing that this most definitely wasn't coming out the way I wanted it to.

"Ruby, please just listen. I wanted you to know how much you mean to me—how I couldn't have gotten through the last few weeks without you, not even close. That you make me feel like the luckiest man alive, even just to be near you—"

"I feel the same way," she interrupted.

"Good, but can you just—"

"Seriously, Ash," she continued, moving away from the door and back toward me, "I can't imagine what I would have done without you."

"Ruby!" I yelled her name, trying to get her to *listen*.

Instead, she jumped backward in surprise. Her eyes widened as her foot caught in the iron bar. She stumbled, her arms flailing outward in the air. I caught her around the waist, holding on for dear life, but it was too late. Most of her body weight had fallen backward, and as I grabbed hold of her, I felt us both falling into thin air.

"ASH!" she screamed, her nails digging into me.

"HOLD ON!" I bellowed, crushing her to me as we free-fell from the tower.

Hexorn, come!

I mentally called the name of the only bird I knew well— the one who had saved me from the earthquake at the Fells. I quietly prayed that he was training with the rest of the flock…

Suddenly I was jerked from beneath, my back slamming into the soft, feathery back of the bird. I heaved a sigh of relief, and looked down at Ruby. She still had her eyes closed.

"It's okay, Shortie. We're safe, it's okay."

"Ash?" She opened her eyes, staring up at me. Her fingers reached out to feel the surface she'd landed on. She inhaled a huge gulp of air when she felt the feathers of the vulture.

"Ash?" she asked again.

"Yes?" I murmured softly.

"What the HELL was that?" she screamed, sitting bolt upright. "Why were you yelling at me? You *idiot*!"

I'd never seen her so furious. She looked as if she was about to rip out my eyes. "I'm sorry!" I pleaded, "I just wanted you to *listen* to me for a moment!"

"Why? What the *hell* was so damn important that you had to knock me off a tower and almost kill me?" she screeched. I got the impression that she wouldn't want me to mention the fact that she was massively exaggerating.

"Because I was TRYING to propose!"

She fell silent.

Finally.

"I want to marry you, Ruby. I want to spend the rest of my life with you. I'm in love with you. Completely and utterly in love with you."

I pushed into the pocket of my robe, pulling out the small gold band that my mother had worn till the day she died. It wasn't much, and it hardly seemed the most fitting engagement ring for an emperor to give his future wife, but it was all I had.

"I don't want an answer now," I emphasized. "Honestly, I want you to think about this, because if you say yes—that's it. I'll never let you go. Take your time."

"Oh, Ash," she sighed, her face lighting up as she reached for my hand. "Even though I'm the biggest pain in the ass?"

"Even though you're the biggest pain in the ass," I confirmed.

I kept the bird circling the castle, finally finding a way that we could spend time together, uninterrupted and in complete privacy. The strange twilight caused by the ripped sky glared behind Ruby's head, making her blonde hair look like some kind of angelic halo, her skin glowing in warm, golden tones as she leaned toward me. I clasped her tightly in my arms, kissing the life out of her—her lips electric, sending volts of desire charging through my body.

"I love you, Ash," she breathed against me. "I love you so damn much."

Ruby

After the vulture had landed, Ash had left me to meet with the ministers and discuss the schedule for maintaining the barrier. I had wandered through the castle on a pink cloud, completely oblivious to what was going on around me. Jenney had enquired after the boys, but I couldn't remember what she'd actually said, or what I'd replied. It was like my feet weren't even touching the ground.

I had always laughed at Hazel's obsession with romance stories—those implausible endings, falling madly in love within a matter of days, reality vanishing in the force of the characters' feelings for one another. I had thought it was the stuff of fluffy fairytales. I had never for a moment believed that

I would ever feel the same way—as swept up by my feelings, as utterly and hopelessly in love with someone who apparently felt the same way.

But marriage?

It felt so sudden.

I quietly shut the door to our room, resting my head on the back of the door and closed my eyes against the strange twilight that bathed the room in pink and purple light. It was peaceful here. I needed to be alone right now, to sort through the conflicting voices in my head. The rational half of me, sounding a *lot* like my father's voice, told me that it was crazy— it was too soon, too hurried. We had insurmountable differences that needed to be discussed before we moved forward together. The other part of me, the emotional part— the sum of my beating heart, the lightness of my body, the shaft of sunlight inside me that felt like it would burst out at any moment—*that* part of me wanted to rush back into Ash's arms and give him the answer he wanted to hear.

What do I do?

Which voice was I supposed to listen to?

The rational side of me had always served me well, had always steered me on the right path. It was the reason I'd survived Nevertide, and why I hoped to make an effective member of GASP one day. I always weighed pros and cons, never taking something at face value, knowing the difference between right and wrong—never allowing room for the gray areas of doubt that so many others suffered from.

But this was different.

Wasn't this the stuff that made life worth living? The unexpected bits, the part where there weren't lists to be made, where there was no right or wrong. There was listening to my heart, and following it to the end just because I could. It was risky, and messy, and there was the danger that my heart could be broken into a million little pieces, the cracks never healing in quite the same way.

It meant change, and in this instance, a fundamental transformation.

A sentry.

An emperor's wife.

Nevertide.

Would he come home with me? And even if he did, would he forever yearn to come back here—and what would he do? He'd wanted to be emperor; he had chosen this. If I was the reason that he left it all behind, would he resent me forever? And what about if it was the other way around? What if I lived here, would I eventually hate him for taking me away from my home, my friends, my family?

Breathe, Ruby, breathe.

I sat on the bed and lowered my head between my legs, steadying the rising panic. These questions needed to be discussed with Ash—calmly. I couldn't solve all our problems in a few minutes, alone.

You love him, just let it go.

I moved, lying back on the soft coverlet. I looked up at the ceiling, noticing the ornate plaster work creating intricate floral patterns, each leaf and vine weaving in and out of one another. I traced the patterns with my eyes, finding the action meditative and soothing.

I did love Ash.

I could say yes, and see where fate led us. Or I could say no, and spend the rest of my life regretting the decision, every day wishing I'd had the courage to submit to the unknown and had enough faith that our love would hold me steady through the journey. I could throw myself into work, my heart slowly hardening, forgetting what it felt like to love and be loved.

I had a simple choice to make, and suddenly the answer felt glaringly obvious.

DEREK

As we journeyed to our destination, we navigated a route that avoided the main roads and thoroughfares which had once been heavily populated—as evidenced by strange hoof tracks and footprints—in order to ensure we remained unseen. We tried to stay under the cover of darkness, as best we could, tracking our route so we remained beneath the patches of sky that had been torn, only showing the pinpricks of stars in the night sky. The good news was that the werewolves were also exposed to a near constant moon, which enabled them to transform.

We had been traveling for an hour before the dragons, and some of the Hawks—Field and his brothers included—stopped us. They had flown on ahead and discovered another deserted castle, one that was fully intact this time.

"Do we stop?" Lucas suggested. "It might be worth exploring—if it's still standing it might give us some better clues as to the types of creatures we're dealing with."

"I agree, let's look into it," I replied, halting the team and changing our direction—veering north instead of east. It wouldn't delay our journey by much, so long as we didn't run into any trouble.

Soon we were following a muddied track, which had clearly been used recently—and by a very large group; there were hundreds of footprints and more of the strange hoof markings.

"What happened here?" Sofia wondered as we walked into a large clearing, a white stone palace in the distance. "It doesn't look like the earthquake damaged it…why would it just be abandoned like that?"

"It looks like it's been empty for a while," I replied, noticing the decay of the building as we moved closer; two walls on the lower levels had been almost completely blown out.

"Derek, Rose." Micah ran up to us. "The kids have been here too. I can smell them. I think recently. The scent's much easier to pick up."

Rose looked around worriedly, assessing the damage of the palace—no doubt trying to imagine what could have happened, wondering whether Hazel and Benedict had been hurt in any way. Claudia pushed her way through the group, followed by Ashley, demanding that Micah direct them to where the scent was strongest.

"Rose." Sofia placed a reassuring hand on our daughter's arm when Rose didn't join them. "This is good news—if the scents are fresh then it increases the likelihood that we'll find them."

Kira caught my eye, then nodded her head in the direction of the forest that surrounded us. My adrenaline shot up uncomfortably. If the werewolf wanted to speak to me away from Rose and Sofia, then I doubted that she had good news to impart.

We made our way out of earshot. Thankfully Rose, at her mother's urging, was heading up toward the palace, along with the rest of the GASP members.

"Derek, there's something I wanted to say, but not in front of Rose," Kira whispered, keeping her voice low. "It's Hazel. Her scent has completely changed. She's definitely still alive," she hastened to add, noticing my look, "but there's something different about her—and I don't know what it is…like her genetic make-up's changed somehow…. but I thought maybe you might be able to prepare Rose in some way. If her daughter's *different*."

My stomach tensed. "And you can't tell what it is? What the change might be?" I urged.

The werewolf shook her head, blonde curls bouncing.

"I'm sorry, I really can't tell. It's just not...human."

I nodded, grateful that Kira had told me alone.

"I'll have a word with her," I promised.

The werewolf nodded before making her way back to Micah.

I didn't know how I was going to broach the subject with Rose. I wondered if it wouldn't be better if I held off till we knew more, but it might be too late by then. I would have to tell her, but gently. When the time was right. At the moment, she was still doubtful that the children were alive—I didn't want to add to that.

"Derek! Ben!"

A shout went up from inside the palace. It sounded like Eli, and I hurried toward the entrance, swiftly followed by the rest of the team. We thundered up the wide staircase, tracking him down. I could tell he'd found someone in the castle. From here I could smell blood and a rapidly beating heart...whatever or whoever it was, they were afraid.

"Through here," Eli called out, and I followed his voice to a door in one of the towers. On the floor in front of him was a woman—an abnormally large, tall woman dressed in a large headscarf and brightly colored, but torn robes. She was crying softly, her hands tied behind her back.

"I've been trying to untie her," Eli said, "but she doesn't

want me anywhere near her."

The woman was slowly shifting away from us on the floor, backing up into her prison. Our presence was obviously terrifying her.

"Okay." I turned to the rest of the GASP members who had followed me in. "Rose, Sofia, Ashley, Grace—please help this woman. The rest of you are going to look around the rest of the castle and the grounds."

The team moved swiftly, giving us some space.

"Do you want me to leave?" Eli asked, evidently wishing that I would say yes. His eyes were wide beneath his glasses, the woman's fraught emotion clearly making him uncomfortable.

"You can leave." I nodded.

Eli heaved a sigh of gratitude and rushed off before I could say another word.

"What happened to you?" my wife murmured softly.

The woman looked at us, her eyes darting across each face as she registered our strange clothes and appearance.

"Who are you?" she asked, her voice trembling. "What are you doing here? Did my master send you?"

Sofia and I glanced at one another. *What master?*

"We're from another dimension," I replied softly, not entirely sure how much I wanted to give away about our origins. The woman didn't look dangerous, but my several centuries of living had taught me that first appearances could be deceptive. "We're looking for some young humans who were taken here, two boys, two girls. Do you think you might have seen them?"

Her eyes rested on mine. I could see she was deliberating about whether or not to tell us the truth—her expression was at once wary and hopeful. I supposed she saw us as her ticket out of this place, if she gave us the right answer.

"Human children were taken for the trials, the kingship trials, by the Hellswans. The ones who locked me up here. Maybe your children were among them…but you're not *human*."

"No," I replied, "not exactly. And neither are you."

She frowned.

"I'm a sentry. Like all the others of this land. Who exactly are *you*?"

Clearly the woman wasn't eager to give much information away until she had a better understanding of what we were. I glanced over at the others again, thinking that perhaps Sofia or Rose should take the lead here. They had more patience than I did.

"We're members of a supernatural organization, created for the protection of humans and other supernatural creatures. We're just here to find our children," Sofia explained gently. "If there's any information you can give us, any at all, it would be really helpful. Maybe you could explain who these

Hellswans are?"

The woman seemed to relax at my wife's explanation, and she nodded.

"I can help you, yes…. The Hellswan family has terrorized this land for years. Tejus Hellswan is the evil, dark overlord who's caused so much of the devastation you've undoubtedly already seen." The woman looked at all of us with wide eyes. "Come to think of it—he kidnapped a girl who looked a lot like *you*."

Her remark was directed at Rose.

"Is she still alive?" my daughter breathed. "And she has a brother too—a small boy? His name's Benedict. Hazel and Benedict? Have you seen them?"

The flurry of questions was answered by an enthusiastic nod from the woman.

"Hazel and Benedict, yes, poor creatures. The last time I saw them was at the trials. They were treated so badly by Tejus and the others. I tried to fight for them—to stop the cruelty to your children and all the others, but look where it got me!" She held up her shackle-burnt wrists, shaking her head sadly.

"Oh, God," Rose gasped. "How were they hurt?"

The woman paused momentarily.

"Have you come across others of my kind before?" she asked, changing the subject.

"No, you're the first," Sofia replied.

The woman nodded again. I could see her mind spinning—whoever this woman was, she wasn't striking me as particularly trustworthy. There was something about her, beneath the eagerness to help and her woeful tale, which struck me as sly and cunning.

"They beat the children badly. They wanted them as slaves to help them in the trials. So many were taken—snatched from their homes in the other dimension…" The woman went on to describe the trials, but I zoned out. I had heard enough. I didn't believe this woman for a second. Why would supernatural creatures, who had obviously gone to great lengths to keep themselves separate from the human world, bother to kidnap children just to be sword carriers and punching bags? No, the woman wasn't telling the truth—and there was something going on here that just didn't add up.

"Where are the Hellswans now?" I asked, cutting through another sob story about the woman's plight at the hands of the evil family.

"They'll be in a castle, one not far from here—Memenion's palace, or Hadalix's, Thraxus's…I'm not sure. One of the royal kingdoms of Nevertide. They left me here to die—they didn't tell me where they were going," she added mournfully.

I nodded. That at least sounded like the truth.

"Rose, Grace, stay here with…what is your name?" I asked.

"Abelle," she replied.

"Stay here with Abelle. Sofia and I are going to discuss what we do from here."

We made our way to the opposite end of the corridor, entering a deserted room. I shut the door.

"I don't trust her for a moment," I stated, waiting for my wife's reply. I knew that I could rely on her above all else to tell me the truth—whether I was being overly suspicious just because the woman was unknown to me.

"Neither do I," she replied. "I don't think she's being completely honest with us. So much of her story doesn't add up…especially about the kids."

I nodded with relief—we were on the same page.

"But," Sofia added, before I could contemplate chaining the woman back up, "I also don't think she's that dangerous. I do kind of feel sorry for her. I don't think we can just leave her here. She's going to have to come with us…if she will."

"I'm not sure I want to give her the choice," I muttered. I wasn't comfortable releasing the woman—she had been chained up for a reason, and though her tales of the evil 'Hellswan' family might well be true, we couldn't know for sure until we found out more. The rest of the castle seemed deserted, so there was no way we could validate her story.

"Dad?"

We both hurried out of the room on hearing Rose's voice. She was where we'd left her, standing by Abelle.

"Abelle has offered to help us get to the other castle—she says the woods are dangerous," Rose said. I knew my daughter well enough to know that she wasn't completely convinced by the woman's authenticity either.

"They are—full of strange creatures that I doubt any of you would have encountered. Nevertide is a dark place, for those who don't know its ways," she murmured coyly.

"Fine," I replied pleasantly. "If you wouldn't mind, it would be helpful to have a guide."

She nodded sagely, lifting herself off the floor. When she stood, I was shocked by her height. She was taller than me.

"We should leave quickly. The Hellswan army has spies everywhere. Nowhere in Nevertide is safe."

As she finished her doom-laden warning, she swept past us, heading back down the staircase. I gestured for Rose and Grace to follow closely, while I hung back with Sofia.

"Do we trust her enough to lead us through the forest?" my wife asked. "I'm concerned that she might lead us into danger, rather than avoid it."

"She doesn't know about the Hawks or the dragons. She's going to get a shock when she realizes we have our own lookout."

"Good point," Sofia muttered. Her worried green eyes glistened with faint amusement. "If she thinks there are strange creatures in the forests, wait till she gets a load of us…"

* * *

Our predictions turned out to be correct.

As soon as the woman stepped out from the castle and caught sight of the army of supernaturals that covered the gardens of the palace, she staggered back in surprise and horror.

Grace and Rose calmed her down, promising that we didn't pose a threat, but the sentry didn't seem convinced.

"Lead the way, Abelle," I prompted, not wanting us to delay our journey any further. The woman scowled, but did as we asked.

Lucas and I walked on either side of her, with Ben behind. The rest of GASP followed us, except the Hawks and dragons who flew on ahead, checking the areas we were about to enter for any possible danger.

"How did you get here?" Abelle asked, once we'd left the grounds of the castle.

"We found a portal on Earth that led us here. It was locked the first time the team went to investigate—and then, without warning, it opened." I kept my answer deliberately vague, but hoped she would have some answers as to why the portal had suddenly opened.

The woman smiled softly to herself.

"The Hellswans locked the portal, making sure that no one got out, least of all the children."

"So why did it open?" I pressed, observing her smile. Clearly she was eager to leave this land, perhaps to travel somewhere the Hellswans couldn't find her.

"I don't know," she replied swiftly. "Perhaps you should ask Tejus Hellswan. I'm sure he knows the reason why."

"Is he a sentry, like you?" I asked, the word sounding unfamiliar on my tongue. I'd never heard of these creatures in all the time I'd been alive. The inhabitants of this dimension had obviously gone to great lengths to keep themselves hidden.

"He is. The cruelest of our kind. My advice to you would be that if you see him, don't hesitate to end him. Nevertide will be forever in your debt if you do."

"Did he do all this?" Sherus asked, gesturing to the sky and the fallen trees we were passing.

"In a way, yes," the woman replied.

Sherus looked at me. I knew he was wondering whether Tejus of Hellswan was the power that had been haunting him—the owner of the mysterious voice that we'd heard in the portal tunnel.

We waited for Abelle to elaborate, but she stayed silent.

I was about to question her again when Lethe flew toward us with the Hawks. They landed, making Abelle jump back in fright. She stared wide-eyed at the icy blue dragon and the winged men.

"We're heading in the wrong direction," Lethe stated. "The

castle is due east. We're veering too far north."

I turned to Abelle.

"My apologies." She smiled. As soon as she uttered the words, her face changed—the woebegone expression of a prisoner vanished, and her lips curled into a malicious grimace. She took out a vial of liquid from her robe, and smashed it down onto the earth where it broke, instantly covering us all with a foggy, foul smelling liquid. It made me feel dizzy and weak, as if my energy was slowly draining from my body.

A horrific, indescribable pain tore through my head. My vision started to blur as I became disoriented, gray and black dots dancing across the scene before me. Sherus, Lethe and Ben all clutched their heads, bent double in agony. Behind us, I could hear the cries of the other GASP members.

I glanced up at Abelle from the ground. Her figure loomed over me. She was laughing.

Julian

"Retreat! Retreat!"

Ragnhild's cry echoed across the cove. I didn't need to be told twice. I was already stumbling over the rocks and sand, heading for the small passage ahead. The feeling that had settled over me on the shore hadn't left. I still felt the icy-cold dread creeping up my spine—the sense that there was something dark and unnatural watching me, waiting to pounce.

It felt strange running from an enemy that I couldn't see, but my imagination had gone into overdrive, and I no longer cared what it was that I was afraid of—even if it was just a feeling. I wanted out of there.

"Julian?" Benedict cried out my name as he ran ahead, pulled along by a guard, checking I was still with him. Yelena was in the other hand of the sentry, the girl slipping and sliding to keep up with him.

"I'm here!" I called back, panting.

Finally, we approached the passage. The guard released them. Benedict rushed through, and I followed, hearing the loud, rapid breaths of more guards behind me. I ran through, scraping my arms on rocks, knocking my shins on rubble, thorns and spiky shrubbery scratching at my face.

Don't stop. Whatever you do, don't stop.

It's coming.

"MOVE! MOVE!" the guards at the rear started shouting, afraid that we'd slow down as we ran single-file up the passage. I couldn't imagine how the last sentry at the end of the line must have felt. How terrified he would be, with no protection between him and whatever it was we were running from.

I heard the bull-horses before I saw them. They had started to whinny and rear up as we approached. They could feel it too.

The guards pulled on their reins, jumping up on the saddles of the bull-horses as quickly as they could. I ran toward our horse, only to see it taken by another guard, who instantly turned and galloped off into the forest.

Traitor!

"Here, boy." A guard grabbed me by the back of my robe, flinging me onto the saddle behind him. Ragnhild did the same with Benedict and Yelena, and a moment later we were all cantering into the gloom of the forests.

We should be taking the path!

I had a bad feeling about this. The forest didn't feel like it was safe territory. It felt like it *belonged* to the force that followed us, somehow, and we were just running head-first into its trap.

We were being followed.

The guards charged deeper into the forest. The small amount of light that had guided us on the way here was swallowed by the trees, till everything around us became black shapeless forms. The sensation of being watched intensified, and as we slowed down to a pace that the bull-horses could maintain, I thought I saw shadows moving out of the corner of my eye.

"I don't like this," my guard grumbled to the other who rode next to him.

"Neither do I."

The other grunted, turning his head around to glance at the troops who followed behind. "We should be moving faster—this place isn't safe."

"Can you see anything?" I asked the guard quietly.

The guard shook his head. "Not a thing. Just the trees…but

the shadows..."

He trailed off, dismissing whatever he was going to say with a shake of his head. It didn't matter anyway—I knew what he meant.

A moment later, one of the bull-horses screamed. The blood-curdling sound was followed instantly by the cry of its rider—an equally horrible howl of pain. The sound came from the back of the line, and instantly the troops broke out in confusion. Some tried to halt their bull-horses from galloping away, while others spurred them on, desperate to get away.

"Stand and fight!" Ragnhild commanded.

The commander rode up to us. My guard was still, holding on to the reins of our bull-horse as it reared and whickered, both rider and animal petrified. I looked around the guard, trying to see what had attacked us. On the floor was the body of one of the other guards, and next to him his bull-horse. One of the trees swayed in the breeze, sending a fragment of light down on the body. He had been disemboweled, his body slashed to ribbons, his insides spilling out onto the dry leaves and soil. His eyes were frozen in horror, wide-eyed and desperate. The bull-horse had met the same fate. The stench of their innards made me heave.

Where is the creature that killed him?

I looked around, squinting into the depths of the forest, cursing the absence of my glasses. I couldn't see a thing, but I could still feel it. Cold, dark, evil. Something was waiting for us.

Another scream went up. This time it came from ahead, from one of the guards who had been prepared to flee.

"Ride!" Ragnhild yelled, changing his command. "I can't see the enemy, we're surrounded. Ride!"

We charged off again, more haphazardly this time, as no guards wanted to be last in line. As we thundered through the trees, I looked behind me.

I didn't know if it was my fear-induced imagination, or the lack of twenty-twenty vision, but I could have sworn that I saw shadows moving across the forest floor—black shapes moving toward us, reaching out to take us into their lightless void.

"Faster!" I screamed at the guard. "Ride *faster*!"

The shadows were gaining on us, inch by inch.

Another rider went down, to the left of us. I watched as the shadows reached out, first grasping at the hind leg of the bull-horse, pulling the creature down with a thump onto the earth. The guard flew backwards. Then came a horrible ripping noise as he was swallowed by the murky shape. I turned my head away. I didn't want to see anymore. We rode on, the screams of the guard still ringing in my ears.

What was that?

I started to hyperventilate, my breathing coming in ragged gasps. We weren't outrunning this thing, whatever it was. We were being hunted down, picked off one by one.

Another sentry screamed up ahead. I looked around for Benedict and Yelena, seeing them about a yard away, their faces ghost white and terrified. Horses reared and screamed, and a second later ours did the same.

"Swords at the ready!" commanded Ragnhild.

The bull-horses started to back up, moving closer together as we slowly became surrounded. The guards looked out into the forest, the darkening pool of the shadow slowly closing in on us with every moment that passed. All I could hear was the short, adrenaline-fueled panting of the guards.

We're going to die.

"Benedict, Julian, Yelena." Ragnhild's voice was low. "I want you to slowly get down off the bull-horses. We're going to charge, and when we do, I want you all to run. You don't stop till you get to the castle, and you don't look back. Do you understand?"

"I-I-I understand." I trembled, looking over at Benedict and Yelena. Benedict gave me a small nod.

"Hurry, boy!" the guard whispered. "Save yourself, and tell the others what's coming!"

I scrambled down from the bull-horse, grabbing Yelena and Benedict by the hand as they rushed toward me. We stood by the edge of the encroaching shadow, waiting for Ragnhild's command.

"On my mark!" Ragnhild called out. "CHARGE!"

The guards stormed forward, the circle of shadow moving from where we stood and racing to meet the oncoming army. I heard the first scream.

"Now!" I yelled, dragging Benedict and Yelena behind me as we rushed into the forest. My legs felt like jelly as I ran, falling and sliding, and then pushing myself up again, terrified of slowing down for a second. The howls and cries of the guards echoed through the forest—not just cries of pain, but of sheer, complete terror—sounds I'd never heard before in my life, and never wanted to hear again.

We kept running. I obeyed Ragnhild to the letter, not looking back once as we headed in the direction of the castle.

"They're gaining on us," panted Benedict a few moments later, "I can feel it."

"I know," I replied, running faster than I thought was possible. "I know."

I sensed the change in the air. It became stale and rank. Horrible goosebumps rose at the back of my neck, turning my blood cold.

Then the whispering started.

Ruby

I looked around me. I must have dropped off to sleep at some point, but I had no idea how long I'd been out for. I walked through to the bathroom, splashing my face with the icy-cold water from the faucet.

Everything felt dream-like, and for a few moments, staring into the mirror above the sink, I wasn't sure whether I had dreamed the proposal or not.

I smiled.

It was real.

Which meant I had something important to do. There was no point prolonging my answer to him. He'd told me to give it some thought, that he didn't want my answer right away, but why wait? I had no idea what the next hour, the next day, would bring.

Rushing out of the room, I slammed the bedroom door shut behind me, wondering where in the castle he'd be.

"There you are!" Hazel was a few doors down, and came hurrying toward me. "Have you seen Benedict, Yelena and Julian? I spoke to Jenney and she hasn't seen them...have you?"

"No, I haven't seen them since yesterday..."

Actually, I hadn't seen them since we arrived. Where the hell were they?

Hazel rubbed her forehead in agitation. There were blueish circles under her eyes, and I got the impression she hadn't had much sleep.

"Don't worry, we'll find them."

Ash could wait. I didn't want the boys wandering around. I didn't know how effective the borders were —having them too far from the castle just wasn't safe.

"When was the last time Jenney saw them?" I asked.

"She said it was when we arrived."

That isn't good news.

"Okay, let's try the kitchens and work from there."

We thoroughly searched the castle for over an hour, calling out their names. We were both getting increasingly desperate. None of the villagers had seen them either, and the guards standing at the entrances to the castle all said the same thing—

that they hadn't seen them since we arrived.

"Let's try the scary hound things?" I suggested. The likelihood of the boys being fascinated with the deadly-looking wolf creatures seemed pretty high.

We walked over to the stables, and found Ash and Tejus talking to a few of the ministers.

"Hey," I interrupted, "have you seen Benedict and Julian, or Yelena? They seem to be missing…"

Ash and Tejus both shook their heads.

"The human boys?" one of the ministers asked.

"Yes! Have you seen them?"

"They left with the recon army," he replied, his face paling as both Hazel and I glared daggers at him. "I thought they'd been requested on the mission. They rode out at the same time as the lieutenant!"

"They're OUT?" Hazel erupted.

No, no, no!

"How did this happen?" I exclaimed. "Why would you think that three young humans would be sent on a mission like that?"

The minister looked to Ash and Tejus for support.

"We just need to go after them," Tejus growled. "Again."

I looked worriedly out to the forests beyond. What the *hell* had those idiots been thinking? Traveling with Ragnhild and the rest of the guards down to the cove? It was about as close to a suicide mission as you could get.

"We need to leave, now," Hazel demanded, glaring at Tejus.

He let out a frustrated sigh.

"Of course. Ash, stay here, I can handle this."

"No," Ash replied firmly, "I'm coming."

Our eyes met.

Thank you.

I squeezed his hand.

"Fine," Tejus replied, clearly displeased. I could understand why; it wasn't exactly the best strategy to jeopardize the life of the emperor for a couple of kids, but I was overwhelmingly grateful that Ash was still putting me and my friends first…and feeling a little guilty.

"Hopefully they won't have gotten far," I replied, looking at the minster for confirmation.

He looked away, staring at the floor. "They were due back before afternoon light."

I looked up at the torn sky. The sun was just after its midpoint.

That's not good.

"Let's move out," Ash commanded. He called over a pair of guards to travel with us, and we all hurried to the stables, saddling the bull-horses. Hazel and I were both riding solo so we had spare rides if we needed it.

"Everyone ready?" Ash called out. When we all nodded, he

ordered the ministers to open the barriers once again. At full speed we galloped out of our protective bubble and headed back to the cove.

"Stay on Ragnhild's tracks," Tejus commanded, leading us down the pathway.

I followed Ash's and Tejus's horses, my riding almost mechanical. I felt like a ball of anxiety, desperately trying not to think the worst. There were a million reasons why they might have been delayed getting back. Ragnhild might have even ordered the kids to get back to the castle, and they had gotten lost on the way.

Please just be lost, I thought to myself, again and again as we continued on our journey.

We traveled along the main road, in the direction that would eventually lead to Hellswan Castle. The cove was a turnoff before that, less well marked, which might help us follow their tracks better. We rode on, neither hearing nor seeing anything amiss until Hazel cried out.

"Wait! Stop!"

We all came to a halt, looking in the direction of the forest on the right of the path.

"I think I can see something… Ash, Tejus?"

They both peered into the forest, using their better-practiced True Sight to make out what Hazel could see.

"It's them," Tejus confirmed, already heading for the forest.

"I can see the red hair of the girl. They seem to be running in the direction of the castle."

We all raced into the thickets. As we got closer, Hazel gasped next to me and I waited for her to tell me what she'd just seen.

"Hang on, Benedict! We're coming!" she cried out, slamming her feet into the flanks of the bull-horse, urging the beast on faster.

Are they in trouble?

I picked up the pace, and after covering a few yards I could hear them calling out to us—desperate and terrified.

Tejus

I jumped off my bull-horse just as Julian flew toward me, his mouth set in a silent scream, his eyes bulging out of their sockets. I looked behind him, but all I could see was Hazel's brother and his friend. Where was the danger?

"Behind us!" Julian gasped out. "We need to leave—now! They're coming, they're coming!"

I caught him in my arms, his entire body trembling with the exertion of the run and his fear.

"Where are the others?" I asked.

"D-dead. Everyone's dead!"

Benedict flew at his sister, dragging her by the arm back to her bull-horse that she'd just jumped down from.

"We have to go!" he screamed.

I kept looking out into the forest, seeing absolutely nothing that could have terrified them so greatly—were they suffering from some kind of hysteria?

Then I felt it.

A cold, dead feeling seeping through my body.

"The shadows," Julian gasped out from my arms, "the shadows are coming."

I looked down at him, gauging from his expression that he could feel the same sick sensation that was pervading my body.

"HAZEL! Get back on the bull-horse!" I cried out, feeling that something was approaching. I didn't know what it was or what Julian meant by shadows, but I understood that we were in grave danger. I could feel it in every cell of my body.

I released Julian, and he ran back to the bull-horses. They were starting to rear and cry, sensing the same danger as we were.

"Ready?" Ash called out, unsheathing the Hellswan sword.

"Ready."

I looked around to see Hazel holding on to Benedict, allowing herself to be dragged back to the bull-horse, but only holding onto the reins.

"Get up, Hazel!" I yelled. She wasn't even looking at me— her gaze was fixed in terror at the forest ahead.

I heard whispering. I wasn't sure if it was inside my head, or coming from the trees, but it was a multitude of indistinguishable voices—all hissing, crying, echoes of dead screams, roars of pain and death. *What is this?*

A great mass of shadow seemed to slither out from the forest floor, growing steadily larger and encompassing the treetops. The whispering increased — becoming louder and more insidious. I thought if I listened to it for another second it might drive me mad.

"Tejus! If the shadow touches you, you're going to die!"

It was Benedict's voice that warned me, just in time. The shadow was slowly growing closer till it was only a foot away from me. I swung out my sword instinctively, and the shadow jerked back. I sliced through air, moving my weapon with practiced motions. Ash did the same next to me, and the guards rushed forward with their swords wielded and ready. We chopped at the dark mass, swinging blindly—the only assurance that we were making any difference was the short jolts backward that the shadow made when it came into contact with our blades. But it kept coming.

I could feel sweat starting to trickle down my forehead and back, my arm growing weary. I didn't dare syphon off Hazel— my only worry was that she wouldn't make it out alive. The shadow was starting to close in on us, the whispers becoming mocking and teasing, laughing at our efforts to destroy them. It wasn't the entity's voice, I knew that much, but it was just as evil.

"Hazel! Get out of here!" I cried again, knowing that she was still behind me. I heard Ash do the same to Ruby, but they didn't pay any attention to us. We were backing up toward them now, the shadow slowly herding us all together.

I moved next to Hazel, forcing her and Benedict to stand behind me.

"Ash, we need to get out of here!" Ruby yelled.

"I know!" he called back, swiping his sword furiously. "But I don't know how!"

I looked around as I slashed my sword. The shadow had almost completely surrounded us. Only a small pool of light on the forest floor was left, the rest was covered in darkness. I held Hazel back with one hand, worried that she'd step out into its gloom. One of the guards screamed. I glanced over to see his body flying up in the air, carried on the shadow as if it were a wave, and then watched in horror as it was released abruptly. His body slammed to the floor. Hazel groaned in repulsion as his innards spilled out—he had been slashed across the chest.

I fought on, slashing more fervently at the black mass.

"It's gaining on us!" Benedict yelled out.

I turned, just in time to see the shadow moving forward, heading for Benedict and Hazel. Before I could do anything, Hazel retrieved her mercy dagger and thrust it into thin air. As she did so, the whispering escalated into a scream. A man's face appeared out of the shadow. It was contorted in a grimace, its eyes nothing but black holes. Its entire form seemed to be created from the shadow itself, only a shade of a man. The figure exploded into a black ash-like substance, floating into the air and then disappearing altogether.

The shadow retreated, but I had a feeling that our reprieve would be brief.

"Everybody leave!" I cried out, dragging Hazel to the nearest bull-horse and flinging her on behind me. She looked dazed—as confused as I was as to what exactly had attacked us. One of the guards grabbed her brother and the redhead. We galloped onto the path, the shadow and the whispering steadily regaining ground.

I held onto Hazel's hands, clasped around my waist.

I had sworn on my life that I would keep her safe, but once again she had been put in the path of danger and I had been unable to fully protect her. What good was my love if it couldn't accomplish that one thing?

I could still feel the sensation of the evil we had left behind. Was that the army that had risen from the sea? An indestructible force that didn't even have flesh in which we could bury our weapons? I had assumed that whatever the entity brought forth would be a force to be reckoned with. But to see something so unnatural, so out of the realm of any enemy I had encountered before, sent another chill racing down my spine.

ROSE

I groaned, lifting my head off the floor.

What happened?

I rubbed my eyes and tried to sit up. My head felt woozy, and I had a headache. I looked over to the still form next to me, relieved it was one I recognized.

"Caleb?" I placed my hand on my husband's arm, urging him to wake up. He opened his eyes, looking up at me in confusion.

"What was that?" he asked, groaning in the same way I had as he pulled himself up. We both got to our feet, looking at the rest of the GASP team, all doing the same—staggering to their feet with baffled looks, some still clutching their heads.

"Dad?" I called, seeing him standing and helping my mother up. "What happened?"

"It must have been Abelle," he muttered angrily, looking around for the woman. It was pointless. Unsurprisingly, she was nowhere to be seen.

"Was it some kind of magic?" I asked.

"I'm not sure what it was... Mona? Corrine? Ibrahim?" he questioned the witches as they approached us, looking *very* annoyed.

"No idea," Mona replied, "certainly the first time I've ever experienced anything like *that*."

The jinn came forward, looking equally irritated that they'd been knocked down by the same magic.

"That was horrible!" Aisha snarled. "What did that bitch do to us? I feel completely drained."

"As do I." Queen Nuriya shook her head furiously. "Where is that rotten creature? She's going to pay for that one day. Mark my words."

"Do you think it was creatures like *her* who damaged the children at Murkbeech?" Claudia asked menacingly, her claws extending.

I nodded slowly. It would make sense. If a human brain was exposed to that kind of treatment it was bound to leave an effect. I wondered if Abelle herself had been involved in the kidnapping of our children?

"I'm going to *kill* her," Claudia raged. "If she's done that to my children—if any of them have—I'll tear them to pieces!"

For once I didn't think Claudia's torture fantasies were an overreaction. I was very tempted to get my hands on Abelle again as well, see how well she fared with a pair of fangs sunk into her neck…

"She'll meet justice," my father barked, "but if she's free, then we need to get to the children before she can warn the army, or get to the kids. Lethe, Azaiah, Field, Blue—will you all fly on ahead and see how far away we are?"

They nodded, the dragons shooting up into the air to join the half-Hawk brothers.

While we waited, I tried to work out how long we'd been out. Maybe a couple of hours? The light didn't seem very different, but it was hard to tell with the massive gashes in the sky.

"I really hope Hazel and Benedict haven't been on the receiving end of that," I muttered to Caleb. "It was so *painful.*"

I shuddered, thinking about them being subjected to the same treatment… perhaps more than once. It didn't bear thinking about.

"I know," he replied with a growl. "I'm looking forward to getting my hands on their captors. They're going to regret crossing this family…"

Corrine walked up to us, placing a hand on my arm. A

second later, the remains of my headache were almost completely gone.

"Oh, thanks," I said, smiling at the witch.

"The same treatment I gave the Murkbeech residents we took back to The Shade," she replied. "It helps soothe the mind."

I felt grateful that when we did find the children, at least we had a team well-equipped to heal whatever they might have endured. I just hoped none of them were in the same state we'd found the human boy who'd known Hazel. He'd been so far gone…

"They're different, Rose," Caleb muttered, as if he'd read my mind. "They're stronger."

"I know," I whispered.

But they're still just kids.

Corrine, Mona and Ibrahim started to heal the others and we all waited impatiently for the Hawks and dragons to return. I started to notice that one benefit of Abelle's mind-attack was that before now, most of the GASP members had been weirded out by the strangeness of the land, baffled as to how another dimension like this could have gone unnoticed for so long. Now they weren't unsettled. They were *furious*. They were ready for revenge, to destroy the creatures that had taken our kids, to fight against a force that could knock us all out like this. We'd be ready for them next time.

Lethe and the others landed, informing us that the castle was a few miles away, still protected by the strange force-field they'd erected around it. They hadn't seen any sign of Abelle.

"Let's get moving," my father commanded.

We continued the journey, moving a bit faster than we had been. As we crossed the floor of the silent forest I heard the quiet and melodic mutterings of the jinn contemplating magic that might repel another attack, and the witches discussing how they might expand the strength of Corrine's mind-soothing skills.

Micah paced ahead, reaching my father.

"We think we can track Abelle, if you want us to try," he said. "She headed off in the opposite direction."

My father shook his head.

"We need you for this. Hopefully there will be time to track her down after we find the kids. I want her brought to justice, but she can't be our priority right now."

"Understood," Micah replied, "but just say the word and she's a dead woman."

I felt a huge swell of pride. I knew that part of this mission was to solve the mystery of the fae king's premonitions and the threat to the In-Between, but I knew deep down that the majority of GASP members were here because of their loyalty to our family—and they were all ready and willing to overcome any obstacle or danger to get the kids home safe.

"Mom, are you okay?" I asked as I drew up near her.

"I'm okay, thanks to Corrine. How are you?" She took my hand, something she hadn't done for a while. It reminded me of being a kid again, feeling so safe when she was around. It made my heart ache. I missed my kids so much.

"I'm okay," I attempted a smile.

"Your father says it's a good sign that Abelle went in the opposite direction—if she's trying to avoid the castle, it might mean that whoever's there poses less of a threat to us. We don't know how much of what she said was lies."

I nodded. It was a possibility, but there was an equally large chance that they were just as dangerous to us as she was, if not more.

"Stop!" my father commanded, pausing mid-stride.

I froze, listening for noises within the forest.

"There are people nearby. Get off the track and up in the trees if you can. They might be heading this way."

The team vanished, melting away into the forest, the jinni and vamps disappearing up into the leaves, the werewolves burying themselves into the undergrowth.

But I stood still.

There was something familiar about the voices…

Hazel.

Hazel.

Oh, God. It was my daughter's voice…

That's my daughter's voice!

It's her!

I started running.

Hazel

"Wait, Tejus." I gripped his waist more firmly. "I think I can hear something…"

We were almost at the castle, and so far we had managed to escape the shadow's approach. The feeling of dread that accompanied the shadow hadn't been felt for a while now, and it seemed that at least for now, we were safe. We had ridden hard, only slowing to a less relentless pace a mile back, giving the bull-horses and riders a much-needed break.

"What is it?" he asked. "The whispers?"

"No…" I hesitated. Was it someone calling my name? It wasn't coming from the direction of the castle though, but from the forest. Had Jenney come looking for us?

"Can you use True Sight?" I asked, pointing in the direction I thought the voice was coming from. "I'm too weak. It's not working."

He looked in the direction of the forest, waving for the other riders to stop.

"What is it, Hazel?" Ruby asked.

"I thought I heard something…"

Tejus put up a hand, silencing me.

"There are people approaching." Tejus leapt off the bull-horse, drawing his sword. Ash followed suit, and so did the rest of the guards.

"Stay on the horse," Tejus warned me.

I heard the voice again. It was definitely calling my name…

My throat constricted. I felt my heart starting to hammer in my chest. With trembling hands, I clambered off the saddle.

"What did I just say?" Tejus barked at me.

I shook my head mutely, lowering his blade with my trembling hand.

"Mom! MOM!"

"Hazel? Hazel, is that you?" The reply echoed across the forest, and a moment later my mom appeared, breaking through the foliage with my dad behind her.

"MOM?"

I thought my legs were about to give way. She ran toward me, knocking me back with the force of her embrace. I smelt the familiar, comforting smell of her—The Shade, the shampoo and conditioner she used, the smell of the laundry detergent we had at home.

"MOM! DAD!" Benedict screamed, and a moment later I could feel his body wrapped in the embrace, followed by my dad. Sobs rocked my mother's body as she repeated our names over and over again.

Eventually, I leaned back—I wanted to look at her face. I still couldn't quite believe that they were real. She smiled at me, taking in my appearance, then looking at Benedict and doing the same. I turned and hugged my dad, who almost squeezed the life out of me.

"What are you doing here?" I asked, laughing. I felt giddy with happiness, like I was in some strange twilight zone. I just couldn't believe that they were really here. Solid. Real. Safe.

"Hazel, you seem so…different," my mother murmured, gazing at me with her warm, loving eyes.

"Yeah, she is," Benedict piped up, "Hazel's now a—"

I jabbed Benedict sharply with my elbow.

"…a badass hero," he finished, lamely.

Jeez.

Now really wasn't the right time to be telling Mom and Dad that! The jab didn't go unnoticed by either of my parents, but fortunately they had also noticed Julian and Ruby in that moment.

"Your parents are going to be so happy!" my mom exclaimed. "Come here!"

Ruby and Julian flew toward my parents, and they got hugs as fierce as ours.

"Where are they? Are they here?" Ruby asked, looking over my mom's shoulder.

My mom laughed, untangling herself from their embrace and turning toward the forest. Seconds later, what looked like the entirety of The Shade's residents appeared, hurrying toward us—Claudia, Yuri, Landis and Ashley were a shooting blur of color.

The rest followed more slowly—the werewolves, the dragons, the Hawks, the jinn and witches, and all the vamps— even my great-grandpa Aiden! I stared, gob-smacked, at all the familiar faces I loved. The faces I had feared I would never see again.

The vamps embraced their children, crying and laughing at the same time.

"Where are your glasses?" Ashley sobbed, tears running down her cheeks as she poked and prodded every inch of Julian.

"And who the hell are *you?*" Claudia had flung herself at Ruby, her arms wrapped around her neck and pulling her taller daughter downward, while she glared at Ash, Tejus and the rest of the guards.

Tejus and Ash looked at one another. Tejus looked

annoyed, Ash dumbfounded. I wanted to laugh at the pair of them. They were in for a treat. The GASP interrogation wouldn't be pleasant for them… *especially* with Claudia being involved. God help Ash.

"We need to get back to the castle," Tejus announced. "We're not safe here."

"Wait a moment." My father frowned. "Who are you and *why* do you have our children?"

I cringed, mid-hug with my grandparents. I had the feeling that things were going to get awkward pretty quickly… and not just concerning Tejus. My hunger had started to flare up, and every time a member of GASP touched me, I was reminded more and more of how unstable I was around non-sentry types… They all smelled so good.

"Mom, Dad, this is Tejus," I said brightly, fighting to swallow down my syphoning instincts.

"Tejus of *Hellswan*?" my father snarled.

"What of it?" Tejus replied, glaring at my father.

Tejus!

I wanted to punch him…I could see that he wasn't going to make this any easier on me or himself—it would be entirely up to me if this situation was going to be defused.

"Dad, look at me," I said, as calmly as I could. "I'm alive— all in one piece. So is Benedict. None of these…err…*people* have harmed us—and Tejus, well—Tejus is my…"

"Boyfriend!" shouted Benedict gleefully.

You're dead.

I made a throat-cutting motion at my brother, but he just grinned back at me. Too much had passed between us. He knew I loved him to the ends of the earth and back, and that he was in no real danger of my revenge. Apparently, all my older-sibling power had vanished.

"Yep!" he cried, over the moon at my parents' horrified faces. "He's our kidnapper as well! She got Stockhouse syndrome... real bad."

"Stock*holm* syndrome, *idiot*," I muttered. "And no, I don't. Anyway, we don't need to talk about this now. Let's get back to the castle?"

I looked over at Ruby for support. She looked as pained as I did; Claudia and Yuri glaring at Ash like they were about to rip his head off.

We needed a diversion, quickly...

"Like hell we will!" my father hissed. "Your kidnapper's your *boyfriend*?"

Oh, man.

I felt blood rising to my face, wishing the ground would swallow me whole. I wished we weren't going through this in front of the entire team either—I could spot Arwen and Grace giggling, and smirks from pretty much everyone else. *Great.*

"What are you thinking?" My father glared at me. Clearly

the 'happy to see my daughter safe' part of the proceedings was over. "And you!" he continued, growling at Tejus so his fangs glinted. "How DARE you kidnap my children! Do you have any IDEA who you've crossed?"

My mom and dad both glared at Tejus. He raised an eyebrow, crossing his arms. If I didn't know him any better, I would think he was completely bored with the exchange. But I could see the clench of his jaw and the darkening of his eyes. He wasn't liking this one bit.

"You arrogant—" my dad burst out.

"Caleb," my mom managed, shaking her head. "Hazel, we'll talk about this later," she warned me. "I mean it. But right now, I'm too happy to think straight… so, Caleb? We're going to put a hold on this for a while. I mean it."

My father growled at Tejus, but stepped back, eyeing him suspiciously.

"Tejus?" I got my 'boyfriend's' attention away from my father. "Let's go back to the castle. Everyone else, you need to follow us. It's not far."

"Follow me," Tejus snapped, leading the bull-horses by the reins. Ash hurried to join him, clearly eager to put some distance between him and Claudia. I couldn't quite hear what she was saying, but there was a lot of snapping and gesturing going on. At least Ash had been Ruby's rescuer initially—*he* hadn't been the one to take her captive.

"Don't say another word," I hissed at Benedict. "I mean it. You're such a massive ass."

Benedict chortled. I tried to frown, but it was so good to hear the sound of him happy. I felt the corners of my disapproving mouth turn up, and turned my head away as we walked to hide it.

"Hazel, I can't believe we found you, alive and safe," she said. "We were so worried. We love you so much – and I don't tell you enough! I'm just sorry it took us so long to get here."

"I know." I smiled. "I love you too. I'm glad you're here. We need your help. The whole of Nevertide is in danger— we've been trying to fight it as best we could, but we need the experts."

"I got that impression," she replied softly, glancing up at the sky.

"Yeah. Things have gotten bad."

She squeezed my arm.

"But you and Benedict are safe—that's the important thing."

I nodded. I just wasn't sure for how long. If GASP had turned up a few days ago, I would have thought our problems were finally over, but after seeing what I had today, I felt differently. I had no idea how we were going to fight whatever that was—the entity's army? The entity itself? There was no way of knowing for sure. But it had scared the life out of me, and I didn't know if GASP would be better equipped to deal with it than we were.

"You do seem different." She smiled at me, brushing a strand of my hair off my face. "But I can't put my finger on it…"

I shrugged nonchalantly, hoping I could put off this discussion till we were in the castle, and maybe even until my parents had warmed to Tejus a bit. Though I wouldn't be holding my breath.

"Maybe it's just because you haven't seen me in a while?"

"Hmm…maybe… You must have a lot to tell me." She eyed Tejus meaningfully.

"Yeah." I smiled weakly. "You could say that."

I'm in major trouble.

Ash

I had never in my life seen anything like the group that stood before me. They had emerged swiftly from the forest, appearing almost instantly—pale creatures, some inhumanly beautiful and deadly-looking, some with wings, and some strange-looking, almost nymphish people who had air where their legs ought to have been.

A short blonde woman, moving at the speed of light, rushed toward Ruby, flinging herself into her open arms. It could have only been her mother. The facial similarities were too evident for it to be anyone else.

So, this is GASP, I thought, trying not to appear too wide-eyed.

"I can't believe we finally found you." Ruby's mother's voice was muffled by her daughter's hair. "I was out of my mind with worry—this place is so strange, and we just kept fearing the worst!"

"I'm safe, Mom, I'm safe. I've *missed* you!"

As the mother and daughter hugged, a man stood by, gazing at them both with disbelief in his expression. He was lean, with a slightly crooked nose, but handsome.

"Dad!" Ruby exclaimed, peering at him from behind her mother.

The man grinned, holding out his arms to embrace his daughter. She hugged him tightly, and I watched a similar scenario happening with Julian—a blonde woman with almond-shaped eyes crying into his hair before scolding him about his glasses.

"Are you sure you're okay?" Ruby's father held her out at arm's length, studying her intently.

"I'm fine, Dad, honestly. I'm just so glad you're here. How did you even get here? How did you find out where they'd taken us?" Ruby burst out with a barrage of questions, practically hopping from one foot to the other as she waited for her father's reply.

"It's a really long story," the man—vampire?—replied.

"We have time." Ruby smiled. "But we'll need to get back to the castle."

The blonde vampire turned to me, moving away from Ruby to glare at me. She stood with her feet hip-width apart, her hands placed firmly on her waist—she looked like she was going to pounce and attack me at any moment. She looked over at Tejus too, then took in the guards and the bull-horses, her eyes narrowing.

I looked over at Tejus, who looked irritated.

"We need to get back to the castle," Tejus announced. "We're not safe here."

It was the wrong thing to say. Hazel's dad started giving Tejus hell. I really didn't want to be in his shoes right now. I braced myself for my own onslaught, glad I wasn't Ruby's kidnapper. Hopefully that would work in my favor, if nothing else did.

"Well?" Ruby's mother glared at me, ignoring Tejus and the other parents and homing in on the person standing closest to her daughter.

"Mom, Dad," Ruby announced grandly before I could get a word in edgeways, "this is Ash! He's my fiancé. Ash, these are my parents, Claudia and Yuri."

Total silence.

I didn't know whether I wanted to shout from the castle towers with joy, or bury myself in a ten-foot grave and save Ruby's parents the bother of doing the job for me. They were looking at me with icy glares. Her mother sneered, showing a gleaming set of fangs.

Oh… This isn't good.

I looked at Ruby, who beamed at me, oblivious to the death sentence she'd just handed me.

"Pleased to meet you." I swallowed, holding out my hand. It remained hanging in the air for a moment, before I dropped it. Her mother was looking from Ruby to me and back again with growing dismay.

At the same time, we overheard Hazel's father shouting, "Your kidnapper's your *boyfriend*?"

Ruby's mother's jaw dropped in shock.

"Please don't tell me you're Ruby's kidnapper?" she growled at me.

"No! No, not at all," I corrected her assumption hastily.

"Ash saved me, Mom. He rescued me, Julian and Benedict from a cellar. We thought we were done for, but thanks to Ash, we escaped unscathed…well, relatively."

"What were you doing in a *cellar*?" her father demanded.

"We have loads to tell you too," Ruby replied. "Nevertide's been… *interesting*."

"Back to the fiancé part," her mother demanded, suddenly less interested in the adventures of her daughter, and far more concerned about what the hell was going on between her daughter and myself. I idly wondered if I wouldn't prefer to be back fighting the shadow.

"I love your daughter," I stated implacably. I wanted them to know that I wasn't messing around—that although this was all obviously coming as a horrible shock to them, my feelings for Ruby wouldn't change no matter what they thought. I was still reeling from her acceptance. The fact that I couldn't touch her without risking losing my limbs was starting to become physically painful.

"And I love him." Ruby smiled at me softly. "There's no better man for me, not in all the dimensions. We're a good team, like you and Dad."

"I find that hard to believe." Her mother crossed her arms, staring at me.

"Well, it's true," Ruby retorted.

It suddenly became crystal clear where Ruby got her stubborn nature from.

"Are you like the others?" Ruby's mother asked me. "A sentry, or whatever you call yourselves?"

"I am," I replied, hoping that Hazel's condition wasn't going to be brought up anytime soon. If they found out what a sentry marriage consisted of, I doubted I'd see daylight again.

"Ash is an emperor," Ruby stated proudly.

"Of this place?" Her father looked around doubtfully. "What happened here?"

"The thing we're running from – or were running from."

I hadn't seen a sign of the shadow for a few miles now. Still, we should be moving. I didn't like standing out here in the open.

Ruby hugged her parents again.

"Keep walking? I just want to talk to Ash for a few moments—just follow that guy." She pointed at Tejus.

"You have mere minutes, Ruby May Lazaroff, then you join us."

Her father's tone brooked no argument. She nodded, smiling and happy, unbothered by her father's obvious disapproval.

We hung back, watching the members of GASP follow Tejus up to the castle. They all stopped to hug, kiss, or playfully punch Ruby on the arm as they went past, exclamations of "Thank God we found you!" and "So happy to see you!" echoed through the group, and Ruby grinned happily at each of them. Tejus took charge, trying to speed everyone up. There wasn't really time for a reunion.

This is who she belongs with.

The thought hit me with complete clarity. This was her tribe—her people. I had the uncomfortable feeling of being separated from Ruby—that I didn't quite fit into her life. The life outside of Nevertide that I'd almost forgotten that she had.

"That was *intense*," I murmured once there was some distance between us and them. I tried to shove the feelings away.

"That's my parents." She sighed happily, laughing at my expression. "They're fierce, but you'll get used to them, and they'll love you. I promise you that. They'll see how good we are together."

I nodded, not quite convinced.

"So," I countered, changing the subject, "you're my fiancée?"

"I am. I decided this morning. I just didn't have time to tell you."

She turned toward me, her face glowing. I leant down toward her, bringing her into my arms and kissing her softly on the lips. It quickly increased its intensity, and just like always, Ruby managed to make the entire world disappear for me—it was only the two of us, in our bubble, the darkness fading away.

"We have a lot to talk about though," she said softly, breaking the kiss.

"I know we do. It's not going to be easy…I'm not blind to the complications, especially now," I said, looking at the retreating members of GASP, "but I swear we can make it work."

"I know we can. I love you, Ash, and that's all that really matters."

I nodded, staring into her clear blue eyes. I hoped she would still feel that way after spending some time with her family and friends. I didn't believe for a second that Ruby was easily swayed by others' opinions—I knew she wasn't. But once she was reminded of her life, her home in the "Shade" place that she'd mentioned, perhaps it would become difficult to hold on to the relationship that we'd built here.

"Here," I said, remembering the ring I had kept in the pocket of my robe.

"Oh, Ash!" Ruby exclaimed as I gently pushed it onto her finger.

"I know it's not exactly fitting for an emperor's wife, but it belonged to my mother. I got it days ago when I went to get my old job back at the kitchens. I thought I would need it at some point."

"You've been planning all that time?" she asked, staring up at me.

"Ruby, the moment I met you I knew. You're the one for me. I wasn't ever going to let you go."

She nodded, tears building in the corners of her eyes. She wiped them away hastily.

"The ring is perfect. I think it's exactly right for an emperor's wife. It's exactly right for *me*."

"RUBY!"

Before I could say another word, her father's voice yelled from the group ahead. Our time was up.

"I'd better get back," she muttered sheepishly. "Just

remember that their bark is worse than their bite…well, except for Mom. Bark and bite are both pretty bad with her, but you'll get used to them."

"Right." I laughed. What else was I expecting? Of course Ruby's parents were going to be tough as nails and slightly terrifying—it wasn't like wallflowers would ever bring up a girl like her.

"Go on," I urged, "before they start accusing me of being your kidnapper."

Ruby ran ahead, snorting with laughter.

ROSE

WHAT?

Dating her kidnapper?

Caleb kept muttering under his breath, trying to rein in his temper, as we followed the sentry my daughter seemed to be infatuated with back to the castle as quickly as we could – trying to keep pace with the slower-moving sentries. I walked between Hazel and Benedict, listening to my son explain the land we were in with an enthusiasm that was totally typical of him—I heard about flying vultures, bull-horses (which explained the strange creatures the other sentries were riding and the hoof prints we'd been finding everywhere), fang-beasts, and the strange mental powers of the sentries themselves.

"They're okay," Benedict explained about the sentries, "once you get used to them—well, some of them are. Some are downright evil, like Queen Trina, and some are just gross, like Jenus."

"Who?"

"Benedict," Hazel interrupted gently, "let's just wait till we get to the castle. Mom will need a proper briefing."

"Yeah, okay—you're right." My son was instantly quiet on the subject, and instead started to question how GASP had managed to get here. I answered his questions, feeling like I truly had traveled to an alternative universe. Since when did Benedict listen to his sister and do as he was asked?

I watched them talk, half involved in the conversation and half watching us all from the outside, still trying to get my head around the fact that we'd actually managed to find them and that they were alive and safe. I could see that they had changed. In Benedict it was subtle, but I could detect a sadness beneath his enthusiasm—a wariness that had never been there before, that should only ever really belong in a person three times his age. I realized that my son had seen too much while he'd been here— they had obviously been through a lot. I'd sent them to Murkbeech for them to have fun and learn survival and team skills. It looked like they'd learnt some harsh life lessons instead.

In Hazel the change was more pronounced, and at the same time, more confusing. Part of it was confidence. She seemed to walk a little bit taller, like she was more solid, more sure of herself. Hazel had always been a daydreamer, part present, part thinking about the latest book she was reading or some fantasy that her head was concocting. I didn't know if it was our sudden appearance or a fundamental, permanent change, but she appeared more present, more in the moment. Was that because of this sentry she was dating? Or something else?

"Hazel, are you all right?" the sentry asked, studying her intently.

"I'm fine," she nodded.

I frowned. Why did he seem to be wary of her interaction with us?

"I can look after Mom," Benedict added, "if you want to go ahead with Tejus?"

"Hazel?" I queried, worried. What was all this about? Why was Benedict watching his sister as if something was wrong?

"She'll remain with us," Caleb snapped.

The sentry ignored us all, watching for some kind of confirmation from Hazel—apparently not convinced by her telling him she was 'fine'.

"Honestly, I'm good. We're almost at the castle."

The sentry nodded, walking on, leading his strange bull-horse by the reins. I bit my tongue. Whatever it was would come out eventually—it looked like I needed to have a long chat with my daughter. There was definitely something going on that I was missing.

Wasn't he too old for her? He seemed like a fully-grown man, and I still considered Hazel just on the cusp of young adulthood. It wasn't just his age that made me skeptical about his suitability for my daughter. He had a darkness about him, not uncommon to supernatural creatures, but he certainly had a 'tortured soul' thing happening: dark, brooding, deadly-looking. A born fighter. That kind of man was in danger of sucking all the light out of my daughter.

From our small interactions so far, he also seemed over-protective of Hazel. And controlling. *Huh.* I tried to ignore the similarities between him and the rest of the Novak men. Was the attraction to kidnappers a genetic thing?

But the Novak men were also brave, good and righteous on the inside—once you got under the hard exterior, despite their sometimes obvious flaws.

Was Tejus the same? I wasn't convinced. I hoped that this thing between the two of them was just a crush, because quite frankly, so far, he'd just come across as an arrogant ass.

"Tejus." Benedict broke off from his chatter, calling out to the sentry in a breathless voice. "I think... I think I can feel it."

"I know," he replied. He jumped up on his horse, turning it around as the creature reared up, and grabbed both Benedict and Hazel, flinging them on behind him.

"Hey!" I exclaimed.

"I understand that your kind has superior speed. Run to the castle and don't look back," he instructed us. "Tell the rest of your team to do the same. ASH!" he bellowed over our heads, catching the attention of another sentry who rode at the back of the line.

"I'm right behind you," the other replied.

The other sentries started to gallop off with their bull-horses. Tejus led the way—Benedict turning his head to look back at us, his face ghost white and his expression terrified. He grabbed the hand of a red-headed girl who I was certain was human, pulling her along with him.

"Let's move out!" my dad yelled to the rest of GASP.

Caleb and I started running after our kids, heading for the castle as fast as we could. The dragons and Hawks flew above us, the jinni appearing every few yards or so and then vanishing, reappearing ahead as they got to know the area. Mona, Corrine and Ibrahim did the same.

As we ran, I started to feel something prickling at the back of my neck—the strange sensation of a million invisible eyes *watching* me.

"Caleb?" I called out, wondering if he could feel it too.

"Just keep running," he replied.

I nodded. Nothing would stop me. Whatever we were running from, I had no desire for it to reach us. It was dark, malevolent and black, like a great abyss was yawning behind me—wanting to consume us all.

TEJUS

The shadows' approach seemed to recede as we neared the barrier to the castle. I watched as the ministers tore an entrance in the enclosure to let us pass. Their eyes widened with shock as they saw the group of vampires, dragons and other strange creatures that made up Hazel's family and friends.

"Let them pass!" I yelled, crossing into the castle grounds.

The ministers nodded, the guards eyeing them suspiciously, hands ready on the pommels of their blades. Ash was right behind me, traveling with Ruby, whom he must have picked up on the way, and the rest of the army—one of the guards had been traveling with Julian.

I swiftly dismounted, turning to help Hazel off the bull-horse. My hands closed around her waist, feeling the warmth of her skin beneath her shirt. She placed her hands on my shoulders for a brief moment as I carried her off, her eyes meeting mine.

"Hungry?" I growled.

I had been worried that she was going to feel the urge to syphon off her parents, and the uncomfortable nod she gave me confirmed it.

"Syphon off me," I murmured, "quickly."

She glanced behind her, watching her parents and the rest of GASP enter the barrier. They were still a little way off, they had overtaken us initially but stopped as they entered the enclosure of the barriers, whereas I'd ridden on to the stables. With the disorder and confusion our new guests were creating with their arrival, she had time.

Her arms moved from my shoulders to wrap around my neck. I pulled her too close, but I couldn't help myself. I heard Benedict and Yelena scrambling off the bull-horse, Benedict making retching noises. Hazel smiled at me, rolling her eyes.

"Ready?" she whispered.

I nodded.

Her lips met mine, her legs wrapping around my waist. I gasped as my energy entwined with hers. The rush was powerful, her syphoning strong and instant. One of her hands moved to the base of my throat, traveling up to my jaw. She tilted my head up higher, taking the breath out of my body. I felt my heart racing, gold threads appearing in my mind—wrapping Hazel closer as my energy fed the void inside of her, filling her till her skin seemed to glow with vibrant, humming power.

Ash cleared his throat.

"Tejus, we need to introduce GASP to Queen Memenion."

Reluctantly, I released Hazel.

"Thank you," she murmured, sliding down the length of my body till her feet touched the floor. The interruption came just in time. Her family was approaching. I focused on Ash, trying to collect myself. My body felt like it was on fire.

I need a cold shower.

"Hazel?" her mother called, beckoning her away. I smirked, turning back to the bull-horse and handing it over to a waiting guard. I had never been in this kind of situation before. As a prince, even one from the most disliked family name in Hellswan, royals and ministers had been desperate for their daughters to marry me—only too happy for me to court them, pushing them my way like they were prized swine. It was a stark contrast to this family, who looked like they happily wished me dead. It didn't help matters that my own conscience in regards to my relationship with Hazel was constantly conflicted. No matter how accepting she was of her situation, and how deeply I knew I loved her, there was always the nagging sense that I had corrupted her—transformed her into something as dark as I was. Watching her syphon off Jenus and feeling her energy become almost polluted afterward had torn at my heart. What a fate and a future I had given their daughter. They were right to hate me.

"Are her parents as big fans of you as Ruby's are of me?" Ash groaned.

"I'm the 'kidnapper'—you'll get off lightly."

"I don't know about that," he muttered, glancing back at the couple I assumed were Ruby's parents. They were openly frowning at the both of us.

"I'm going to get Queen Memenion and Jenney. They might be able to defuse this…and then we need to talk about what the hell we witnessed in that forest." Ash shook his head, as baffled as I was.

"We need to talk to the Impartial Ministers," I added. "I want them at the meeting. There's a minute chance that they'll be able to shed some light on what that thing was—or *things*." I still wasn't sure whether the shadow had been one large malevolent force, or some strange multitude of creatures.

"Agreed. They've been avoiding us ever since we arrived. It's time they were of actual use."

With a heavy sigh, Ash began escorting the members of GASP to the castle. He avoided making eye-contact with Ruby's parents. I laughed to myself. He wouldn't get away with it that easily.

I hung back, deploying an avoidance tactic of my own while I thought more about what we'd faced today. The fact that it had seemed completely immune to our swords terrified me. The only victory that we'd had was when Hazel had stabbed the form. Was it because she had managed to come into contact with something? Or was it because of the dagger that she'd used? I'd never heard my mother or her family mentioning that the Mercy Dagger contained any specific qualities that would make it any different to our weapons. Deep in thought, I wandered over to the castle entrance, relieved to see that GASP had ventured inside. The coast was clear.

"Tejus?"

Or not.

A man stood by the door, watching me. He had black hair, contrasting dramatically against skin much paler than my own. His blue eyes were intense, meeting mine as if he could see right through me. He looked young like all the rest, but as I met his gaze, I wondered how old he truly was. There was something that made me think that he had seen many lifetimes before this one.

"Yes," I replied as politely as I could.

"I heard about you before we arrived here."

I nodded. That wasn't unusual—if they'd met a passing traveler who had rejected the confines of Memenion's palace, they would undoubtedly mention me…and damn me.

"I'm not a very popular man."

The man arched an eyebrow in my direction.

"That's putting it mildly," he replied sardonically. "It was a woman named Abelle. We unchained her from a tower, only to be thanked by her later — knocking us out, en masse, as we traveled through the forest."

So she's escaped.

"Bravo," I bit back. "She was a prisoner. She was in league with the Acolytes, a cult dedicated to bringing about the rise of the creatures that chased us just now."

"And you left her in a tower?" he hissed back, not taking kindly to my sarcasm.

"We had no choice. She was a liability—better that she rotted in there."

I didn't tell the man that she had harmed Hazel, had tried to get her killed. It would undoubtedly bring up more complicated subjects that I wasn't willing to discuss till Hazel and I had a chance to decide how best we would tell her parents.

"How much of a danger is she now?" he asked.

"I can't be sure. The rest of the cult is dead, and they have achieved their aim. Perhaps she is useless to the entity now, I have no idea."

"It seems we have a lot to discuss," the man replied, contemplating my response.

"Ash, the emperor, will be holding a meeting. Perhaps you should find sleeping quarters and prepare yourself for what lies ahead," I replied. *And stop questioning me.*

"I am not finished with you yet, Tejus of Hellswan. I take it you are the man involved with my granddaughter?"

Ah.

That's who he is.

"Yes," I sighed, readying myself for another onslaught.

"Hazel comes from a long line of Novaks. Our family is powerful, our history darker than you could possibly imagine. I trust that your intentions are honorable?" His last line was laced with malice and an underlying threat.

"They are, sir."

"You would have quite a force to be reckoned with if they were not."

"I am well aware of that," I replied, keeping my temper in check. "But I love your granddaughter. This is not something I take lightly, and I do not love her carelessly. Hazel may be part of your bloodline, but she is also part of my soul. Try to take her away against her will, and you will become acquainted with my equally unpleasant and powerful family."

He didn't have to know most were dead, and one was chained up beneath the castle.

"That's not my intention," the man growled, "but I love my granddaughter, and I am having a difficult time understanding what she would see in you."

"I don't blame you," I replied quietly. "But that is not my concern. For whatever reason, Hazel loves me—and I'm honored that she does."

The man nodded, quiet for a few moments. I sensed that I had passed some kind of test, and for now it seemed that he wouldn't be questioning me any further. No doubt that would change once he understood what I had caused her to become, but I would have to face the consequences of that when the time came.

"This...*protection* around the castle. What is it?" he asked eventually.

"Barriers. They're created and upheld by the mental energy of the sentries—our ministers usually attend to that task. They have more developed powers than guards or laborers."

"How do sentries come by this mental energy?"

"We feed on energy—of our own kind, and other creatures."

"Like humans?" he shot back.

Damn.

"Yes, like humans."

"Which is why you kidnapped the children from Murkbeech?"

I nodded, wondering how best to explain our actions.

"We had trials, to gain the crown of Hellswan. My father instructed that my brothers and I portal to Earth and collect those whose minds were strongest. In the past it has been an uncommon practice. Most of our kind don't wish to travel between the dimensions, preferring to disassociate ourselves from humans and other supernaturals—some of which, till today, I hardly believed existed. But the minds of humans are rich in energy, especially when they are young, and especially when they are flexible—like your grandchildren and their friends. I believe it is their acquaintance with the supernatural world that has caused their superior mental energy."

"Does it cause them pain when you feed off them?" he asked, getting to the heart of his concern.

"It can," I replied honestly. "But your daughter found a way to syphon without causing pain to the humans. Now that has become the common practice among my kind when syphoning off humans."

"She's smart, like her mother," he muttered. "Do you still 'syphon' off Hazel?"

"Not often." I cleared my throat, hoping that he would change his line of questioning.

"Tejus?" Hazel appeared around the doorway. On seeing her grandfather, she smiled broadly, but it dimmed as she fully registered both our expressions. "Grandpa, I'm going to borrow Tejus for a moment, is that okay?"

"Of course," he replied, his mood instantly warming as he turned to his granddaughter. "I'm glad to see you're safe, Hazel."

I nodded my goodbye, and he returned it, his eyes back to watchful and mistrusting—but I felt like I was making progress. He no longer looked as if he was imagining ripping my throat out.

"I'm sorry," Hazel whispered as we ascended the main staircase. "They'll lay off you soon. It's just new to them…you're my first boyfriend, and, well, you know—you're a sentry. It's a lot."

"I understand that. Don't worry about me, Hazel," I chided her gently, "I'm perfectly capable of conversing with your family."

I allowed myself a small smile at her admission that I was her first boyfriend.

"What?" she asked, catching me.

"Nothing."

"Right," she drawled.

"Where is everyone else?" I asked, wondering how much time we had until Ash called his meeting.

"Getting settled, I guess," she replied with a shrug.

I lifted her into my arms, carrying her up the last two steps.

"What are you doing?" she exclaimed, half laughing, half admonishing me with a glare. Without answering, I prowled the corridor, trying to locate our room. The door was ajar, and I pushed my back against it, letting us in, then kicked it shut.

"Finishing what we started," I replied hoarsely.

"They're right—you're a *terrible* influence." She smiled, biting her bottom lip.

My hands ran over the curves of her body, our breathing

rasping and desperate. She caught my lips in a kiss, her hands entangling themselves in my hair as she urged me closer. I looked into her eyes, stroking the porcelain skin of her jaw with my thumb. I was humbled by the love I saw looking back up at me.

How do you feel this way about me? I wondered, not for the first time.

"Hazel," I groaned against her. Our kiss intensified, our lips molding, our inhales and exhales coming in perfect unison.

"I need to know," I rasped, breaking the kiss but not moving, our lips an inch apart. "Do you have regrets about becoming a sentry, still?"

"No," she answered without hesitation. "It makes me feel like you're a part of me. I wouldn't change it for all the world."

I nodded, speechless. My throat burnt, aching with the unspoken weight of devotion I felt for her in that moment.

"Hazel?" A now-familiar voice spoke sharply from the door. I turned, Hazel scrambling back down to the floor, and saw her mother standing in the entrance, glaring at us both. Clearly I hadn't shut the door properly.

"*Mom!*" Hazel gasped, looking mortified. "Awkward!"

Awkward indeed.

JENUS

I heard the clatter of the trap door being opened. Two guards were already waiting down below with me, playing a card game. I could smell the food before I saw the sentry who was bringing down my dinner.

It was later than usual, and along with the absence of the three other guards who usually spent the day down here, I suspected something was going on above. Perhaps my master? Perhaps his children, coming to wreak pain and oblivion on the foul insects that ran amok in this castle. I had tried to use True Sight earlier in the day, but with such depleted energy, I could only make out hazy shapes of gray above me—nothing to indicate that rescue was on its way.

One of the guards gestured to the other that he should open the door. They were the younger of the sentries that had been posted to watch me. I watched as a servant girl stepped out of the gloom and walked toward me, her eyes fearful. I recognized her from Hellswan castle. She had been one of the servants there, and was as thick as a tree stump.

The guard tore the barrier, allowing the girl to place the food between a small, oblong slit at the bottom of my cage. She did so hastily, but before she could withdraw I reached out, swift as a viper, and grabbed her wrist, yanking her against the bars of my cell. Instantly the guards started to syphon off me, but they couldn't do it as forcefully or as effectively as I could to the young servant girl. Her energy was delicious, sweet like berries, and she smelt of sunshine.

"Stop! Stop! Please," she whimpered, her beautiful blue eyes rolling back into her skull.

"Jenus! Stop instantly!" one of the guards bellowed. I paid him no heed. Once I was full of her, I released her arm and she fell backward onto the stone floor. The guards began to re-build the barriers, moving the servant girl out of the way.

"No, you don't!" I laughed. I started to syphon off the both of them, draining them as quickly as I could. With a heavy thump the guard holding the keys fell to the floor, and then the other followed, howling out with pain.

I stood up, enjoying the surge of energy that ran through

me.

It was short-lived. A moment later, the hatch to the room was torn off. Guards clattered down the stairs, the broadswords clattering against the stone walls as they surrounded me.

"Back!" I screamed. "BACK!"

Most of them laughed at me, simultaneously syphoning all the energy I had just gained. I tried to reverse it, to take from them what they were taking from me, but it was no use. There were too many.

The servant girl was cradled in the arms of one of the guards, who looked up at me in disgust.

"Don't think you'll be getting fed for a long time, Jenus," one of them said as the ground rushed up to meet me.

"You will pay for this," I spat, growling on the floor. "My master will come—come and destroy you all. You will regret the day you were dragged from your mother's wombs! I will END you!"

"I think it's starting to get to him," one of the guards muttered to the other.

"Nah. He was always mad. Always missing a piece." The guard tapped his head, laughing at me.

Fool!

How dare he laugh at me? How dare my brother subject me to this mockery? Didn't he care that by tarnishing my name, he hurt his own? How would his people respect him if they continued to disrespect me?

I lay helpless on the stone floor of my cage, every bone in my body hurting, my head feeling like a million ice pricks were piercing into the soft tissue of my brain.

Master…why have you forsaken me?

Was this to be my future? Would I have to wait here till the end of days, never able to prove myself worthy of my master's love? What then? Would I still get the rewards I had been promised? I doubted it.

"We'll get some ministers down here…prevent him from doing this again. And no more servants—guards only. Make sure the barriers remain strong in the meantime."

"Will do," the other said.

"I can promise you riches!" I cried out before the barriers could be erected. "I can promise you a life beyond your wildest dreams!"

"What? Like the one you're living?" The guard burst out laughing.

"My master, he will be here. He will come and you never need work for another man again. You will be a *free* man!"

The guards just laughed harder, and carried on putting the barrier in place.

Justice will be swift, I promised myself. *When my master rescues me, justice will be swift and merciless.*

As I laid my head back on the floor, I realized that my

impulsive actions had perhaps ruined my only viable escape route. Tejus would never let Hazel down here with just the two of them when he heard of this. Not unless his arrogance let him believe himself completely omnipotent. Perhaps there was still a chance. No doubt his ego grew every day that his ex-human believed herself to love him.

Brother, come to me, I prayed. *Come believing you are invincible so that when I take you down it is that much harder to bear.*

BENEDICT

The meeting had been called, and for once I had actually been asked to attend. I'd *known* our joining Ragnhild's mission would pay off. Though it was only because the rest of his army was dead that Julian, Yelena and I were the only ones who knew what had taken place at the cove—maybe I shouldn't gloat too much. But it was exciting—having GASP here, knowing that we had an unstoppable force that was going to come up against the entity. I couldn't wait for them to come face-to-face with the evil that had possessed me and made my life completely miserable and terrifying for so long. If the entity thought it was great and all-powerful, wait till it met my grandpa.

"Julian, Benedict, can you tell us about what you saw at the cove?" Ash asked, interrupting my vengeance fantasies—fighting side-by-side with Grandpa and the rest of GASP, me wielding a sword like a pro.

All eyes turned to me, Lucas trying to hide a smirk. I looked to Julian for backup. He frowned at me, urging me to speak. Julian always disliked large groups.

"Well, we saw the bodies of the Acolytes," I replied quietly. "And some weird energy barrier covering them—like something was sucking their energy, creating a sort of force field."

"All the energy was going into the earth…that's what it looked like," Julian added.

"A conductor," Yelena interrupted. "Obviously, the entity is using the bodies of the Acolytes to syphon off their energy to rise up—my guess is so he can become whole, so he can fight us."

Smarty-pants.

"Okay," replied Ash, smiling warmly at Yelena, "that's a likely conclusion to draw—unless the shadows that we fought today are the entity itself?" He looked to Tejus, who shook his head.

"I'm not sure about that. I believe the shadow is the army that the book predicted. Yet because Hazel killed Queen Trina, I think we have bought ourselves some time. I don't believe he is fully risen yet."

"Who did Hazel kill?" my mom exclaimed.

I looked at my sister. She seemed uncomfortable.

"Our enemy," I replied. "She was amazing. Wasn't she, Tejus?"

The sentry smirked. "She was."

"I think someone needs to bring us up to date with what's been happening," my grandfather said. "We are playing catch-up here and I need to understand what's taken place. Sherus." He turned to a copper-haired fae I'd never seen before. "Does this entity sound like it could be related to your visions?"

The fae nodded, eyeing the sentries with suspicion.

What's his deal?

I'd never seen him around The Shade before. I leaned back into my chair as Ash and Tejus told GASP what had been happening and explained a bit about the abilities of the sentry species. To hear it all laid out, it sounded like some kind of bizarro fairy tale. I had a hard time believing it myself, and I'd been there! Every so often, my mom and dad would turn to me with panic-stricken eyes. To be honest, I'd been hoping they'd be more impressed with our brave deeds—but they just seemed worried. My grandpa also told us about the entity whispering to them as they passed through the portal. It seemed like he was *everywhere* at once, and the thought scared me—to communicate to them through a portal like that? It would have taken a lot of power.

"I can't believe you've been through all of this," my mom whispered when Ash and Tejus had finished.

"We're *fine,* Mom," I groaned, seeing Yelena stifling a giggle out of the corner of my eye. I'd like to see *her* parents act any differently. They'd react way worse—they weren't even supernatural!

"Has it occurred to you that there might be jinn in Nevertide?" my grandfather asked Tejus.

"It has," Tejus bit out. Now it was my turn to hide a smile—watching Tejus get it in the neck from my family was *awesome.*

"The threat of the entity rising delayed our plans," he continued. "But if there are jinn here, they are well-hidden. I have not come across your kind"—he looked at Nuriya, Aisha and Horatio—"and before reading the book I had no knowledge of your existence."

"Have you had any more luck in sensing anything here, in Nevertide?" my grandfather prompted the jinni queen.

"No, I've felt nothing, but it doesn't mean that they're not here. Jinn can cloak themselves well, if they don't wish to be found. It's unlikely we'll just stumble across them by chance," Nuriya replied. "Also, the jinn are the only creatures that would have been able to create those stones. But if they are not emerging now to re-bind the creatures contained within, perhaps they no longer reside in this land?"

"We should seek them out," Uncle Ben replied. It was the

first time he had spoken during the meeting, but everyone instantly paid him attention, even Tejus. He was just like that—a born leader, just like my grandfather.

One day I'm going to be like that, I promised myself.

"What about lands beyond the water, would they find a home there, perhaps?" the jinni queen questioned Tejus and Ash.

"We don't know what lies beyond the ocean," Ash replied, clearing his throat. "We don't travel there. None of our kind do. We use the portal if we wish to visit the human world."

"You've never been curious?" my grandpa asked.

"Nothing lies beyond it," Tejus snapped. "Ocean as far as the eye can see. We have True Sight. We know there is nothing more to be found."

The GASP team looked at one another in confusion, bewildered how Nevertide could be a dimension all of its own. I couldn't make sense of it either. I looked over at Hazel, who shrugged.

The conversation moved swiftly on.

"By your accounts, this shadow is impossible to kill. It doesn't look like we have many other options available to us," my uncle continued.

"*Near* impossible," Hazel corrected him. "When we were fighting them, my dagger definitely came into contact with something—almost like it burnt part of the shadow. It was weird, but the rest of it backed off. It's how we were able to get away."

"Do you have any theories?" Tejus prompted her.

Hazel hesitated before replying. I realized she was just as nervous as I was about talking in front of the sentries and GASP.

"When I first saw the water that the Impartial Ministers were using to regenerate themselves, I couldn't help notice how similar it was to the stone in my pommel. I don't know why, but I think it has something to do with that."

"Show me your dagger," one of the Impartial Ministers commanded. Simultaneously, Tejus and my dad turned and glared at the wrinkly sentry.

"Show some respect," Tejus snapped.

Hazel ignored the tone of the Impartial Minister, laying her dagger on the table. It was one of the most amazing weapons I'd ever seen—I'd coveted it since I saw it. I hoped Tejus had a few more to spare.

"Let me see that." The fae took it from the table before the Impartial Minister could. He studied the dagger curiously, paying particular attention to the stone at the end of the handle—it looked like a marble or something, but almost like it was *alive* inside. So cool.

"Sherus?" my grandfather questioned. "Is this something you recognize?"

"This is no stone," the fae replied quietly. "This is a glass vial, and contained within it are the waters of *immortalitatem*—the water the jinn gifted our kind long, long ago."

The Impartial Minister looked furious, though I couldn't understand why.

"It is the water of the Impartial Ministers!" he exclaimed. "We created the immortal water!"

Queen Nuriya gave a snort of derision, and the old sentry glared at her.

"You, yourself?" Tejus questioned the Impartial Minister slyly.

"No, of course not. It was created long ago by our forefathers."

"But you don't know for sure?"

The Impartial Minister looked affronted that Tejus would doubt him. I sighed. Of *course* the jinn would have made it—like the Impartial Ministers would ever create anything remotely helpful.

"Whoever created it," my grandfather interrupted diplomatically, "it obviously has properties that might benefit us, if Hazel is right. Is this immortal water mentioned in any of the literature you mentioned earlier?"

"No," Tejus replied. "But if it is also created by the jinn, which I imagine is likely, then perhaps it is another weapon we can use against them."

"A weapon!" the Impartial Minister burst out. "The water is sacred, it is *not* a weapon!"

"Someone might mistake you to be on the side of the entity," Tejus replied dryly.

"We are just trying to maintain order!" the minister replied.

"Order is gone," Tejus barked back. "I don't know if it's escaped your notice, but Nevertide is in tatters and many of your kin are dead. If we all die, who will be left to keep your precious order?"

"You have always been unreasonable, Tejus," the old minister replied, looking like he was sucking on a lemon.

Tejus turned back to the rest of the table. "We have the water; we just need to work out a way we can use it and test Hazel's theory."

"Get us to the water, and we can do the rest," Ibrahim announced.

Tejus looked at Ash, who nodded.

"We leave at dawn, and we'll avoid the forests as best as we can," Ash asserted. "Everyone get some food and get some rest."

The room started to empty.

"I don't think we've met yet?" My mom came up to Yelena, smiling down at her. "Were you kidnapped from Murkbeech?"

"No—Rome. I was on holiday with my parents when I was taken," she replied cheerily.

"I'm so sorry." My mom looked horrified.

"Don't be." Yelena shrugged. "I like it here—well, I like being with Julian and Benedict and the rest of the kids. It's been fun. My parents were just going to send me to boarding school at the end of the summer holidays, so it doesn't really make a difference to me. The food hasn't been great though." She pulled a face.

"Oh."

My mom looked impressed. I guessed in some ways Yelena was kind of like a GASP member in training—even though she'd told me she was always afraid, you'd never know it. It would be kind of cool to have her back at The Shade—maybe for holidays. Not full time though. She would drive me *mad*.

"You should also know that your son saved me from a burning building," Yelena continued, "no one mentioned that bit when they were debriefing you. And then he saved me from Acolytes when they tried to kidnap me and take all my energy. Then he saved me again today, dragging me back from the cove when I was so scared I thought I wouldn't be able to move."

She said it all so matter-of-factly, like it was no big deal—but when she was finished her eyes looked a little glassy, like she might start crying.

"He's an amazing boy," my mom whispered, hugging her.

"He is," Yelena agreed, burying her face in my mom's hair. *What's going on?*

They were getting weirdly emotional—and completely ignoring *me*, the hero of the story! I rolled my eyes and left the room.

Honestly.

Hazel

I caught up with Tejus after the meeting. GASP and the sentries who had been present were piling out into the hallway, trying to relocate their rooms.

"Thanks for your support," I murmured. "Do you think the water's really the weapon that's going to stop these creatures?"

Tejus looked at me. There were dark shadows under his eyes, and the glow from the candles made his cheeks look more gaunt than usual.

"I really hope so. I don't have any other ideas."

"Me neither. I always thought that if GASP ever came all our troubles would be over. I guess it was naive of me to think they'd just wave a magic wand and all this would go away."

Tejus smiled at me gently.

"No. It's good that you have faith—in your family, your friends. It's just not always as easy as that. I wish it were."

I nodded. Me too. My mom brushed my arm, getting my attention. She was standing with my dad, both of them looking beat.

"Get some rest," I said, hugging her tightly. "I'm so glad you're here."

"Me too. I'm so proud of you and Benedict, Hazel."

I said goodnight to my father, though it was only really dusk—the sun hadn't completely set for the day, but with all that had happened in the last few hours, we all needed time to reset.

As they walked off my father whispered, "Where is Hazel sleeping? They're not sharing a room yet, are they?"

I turned, cringing up at Tejus.

"He has a point."

"Don't start." I shook my head. Tejus was as old-fashioned as the rest of them, but there was no way I would be parted from him—not tonight, or any other night to come.

We started to climb the staircase. On the second step, I paused, feeling a cold sense of dread unfurling in the pit of my stomach. I clutched the banister, suddenly feeling alone—like the candles had been blown out, the crowd of people gone, the hallways and rooms empty, echoing husks.

"Tejus?"

"I can feel it," he replied, his hand taking mine. The touch brought me back to reality, but the fear was far from gone.

"*Where* is it?" I asked.

Without replying, Tejus grabbed me by the arm. We raced over to the front door. As we passed the crowd, everyone had gone quiet, frozen in their own, singular nightmares. We could all feel it.

"It's coming."

Benedict was standing in the doorway that led from the banquet hall, rooted to the spot – his eyes wide.

"He's coming."

Tejus pushed open the front doors. The ministers were still at their posts, surrounding the barrier. The guards all stood by their tents, the villagers too. They were all gazing up at the sky.

It looked just like it had before the meeting—the pinks and purples of the sunset blazing on the horizon, the blue of the sky moving from light to navy ink the higher it got.

Where are you?

The crowd had gathered behind Tejus and me. We slowly stepped out onto the terrace, our eyes searching the landscape, looking for the danger that we could feel. Remembering what Ash had said in the meeting, I kept my gaze fixed on the forest. It was so dark it was difficult to see. Aside from the very tops of the trees that were softly bathed in what little light we had left, the thickets of the forest were a little more than a black, indistinguishable mass.

Then the blackness started to move.

"It's coming from the trees," I breathed.

It moved so silently and fluidly, at first I thought it was my imagination. But the dark shadows of the trees had slowly seeped over the lawn, inching its way toward the barriers.

"Ash!" Tejus barked, making me jump. "We need more sentries and guards. Everyone, secure the barriers!"

The ministers already working jumped to attention, refocusing themselves away from the creeping horror to the strengthening of the only protection we had.

"I need to go down there and help. Stay here and be with your family?" Tejus turned to me, his dark eyes fixed on mine.

"No. I'm helping you. I'm a sentry. I can help maintain the barrier, and so can the witches from The Shade."

Tejus growled, yanking his hand through his hair. Ash and the remaining ministers were already rushing past us down to the borders. "At the first sign that it might collapse, you run inside. Do you understand me?"

"I understand you."

He nodded sharply. "God help me, Hazel—I'll pay for the danger I've put you in one day."

I ignored him and we ran down to where the other ministers and guards were standing. It wasn't true that Tejus put me in danger—the first kidnapping instance, maybe, but after that it was all my own doing. I'd chosen to fight.

"Everyone spread out! Cover as much ground as you can!"

Tejus barked out commands, his voice splitting the cold evening air. I watched as he marched over to the witches, asking for their help. The sensation of dread and fear was getting stronger. I felt almost crippled by it—like a hand was grasping tightly at my heart, clamping my organs still. I was having difficulty breathing, my lungs and throat grabbing at the thin air.

At Tejus's command, I lifted my hands up and closed my eyes. I tried to find the ball of energy I knew would be inside me, the bright light that was now part of me. The fear was distracting. I tried to ignore the spidery clutches of terror running across my body, concentrating on imagining energy, light—

There you are.

I found it. With everything I had, I threw the energy outward. Its electricity left the tips of my fingers, feeding itself as it dispersed, growing brighter and more brilliant inside of me.

I opened my eyes.

It was working. I could almost feel the barrier becoming stronger, its translucent skin building itself, becoming thicker and more solid.

I looked over at Tejus. He was standing to my left, his eyes fixed ahead as the shadows became longer, slowly working their way up the barrier, casting all of us in their darkness. His mouth was set in a grim line, and were it not for the slight tremors that ran through his muscled frame, I would have thought that this was costing him no effort at all. His face, the pronounced cut of his jaw and cheekbones, had almost entirely been swallowed by the gloom, but his eyes, as black as onyx, seemed to blaze like a cat's in the dark.

"Hold steady," he whispered.

I turned my gaze back to the barriers. The shadow was still lengthening across its surface, but I could feel our protection working. The horrible, fearful sensation was still present, but it wasn't growing, it couldn't hurt us.

Then the whispers started.

Low and indistinguishable, the voices felt like they were coming from the inside of my head—purring, curling soft sounds that should have been gentle, but were so discordant and filled with malice that I thought I'd go mad if they continued. My energy wavered, the gold light inside of me dimming.

"Hold on. Listen to my voice, Hazel!"

I swallowed, trying to tune into Tejus, like sorting through radio frequencies.

Stop! Stop whispering to me!

"It's just sounds, they have no power over you. I know it sounds like they're inside you, but they're not, they're just voices." Tejus talked to me, his voice jagged and desperate, willing me to hold on.

It wasn't just me who was slowly losing the will to fight back. I could feel the barriers becoming thinner as the rest of the sentries tried and failed to keep the whispering at bay.

We needed more energy, more light.

"Mom! Dad!" I called out into the darkness, hoping that they weren't far away.

"We're here, Hazel—what can we do?" My mom answered me. She was only a few yards away—she and the rest of GASP must have stood by, watching the sentries and witches work, powerless to do anything else.

"I, we, need your energy—all of you. Will you let us syphon?"

"Anything. What do we do?" my father replied, sounding confused that I was somehow performing the same magic as the rest of the sentries.

"Just be willing," I replied. "Tell the rest to do the same— each of you, as close as you can behind a sentry. Hurry!" I felt my light dimming.

A second later, my mom reached out and touched me gently on the shoulder.

"I'm here, Hazel."

"I'm sorry I didn't tell you before," I whispered.

She didn't say anything, but I felt her grip tighten on my shoulder. I closed my eyes, letting the hunger consume me, reaching out for my mother's powerful energy. It was so pure and bright, just like Ruby's was. As my energy leapt out to meet hers, I felt an outpouring of love, warm and comforting, flowing freely toward me—unconditional and as pure as her energy. I swallowed, feeling a lump in my throat. Of course, I had always known that my mother loved me, but to *feel* it, to have it cover me—smelling like our home, the trees in The Shade, the salt water from the sea—it made my heart ache.

I could see my dad and Benedict standing behind Tejus. They weren't touching, but I could see that Tejus was growing stronger, feel the impenetrable wall of his energy growing strong.

It's working!

The barriers started to thicken again. So powerful was the energy of the GASP members and the witches that were assisting, that the barrier was no longer translucent. It started to almost glow—a faint white hue coming off it that made me think of the immortal waters, and a sense that whatever gave the water its rejuvenation or healing properties, it also cleansed, washing away whatever darkness there was in this world.

Tejus turned toward me and smiled.

"Vampire energy?"

"Yep." I grinned back.

"Impressive."

"You're welcome," my father growled sarcastically, sounding *very* unsure about Tejus feeding off him. I guessed that most of the vamps would be disturbed by the sudden role-reversal.

The whispers had intensified, growing colder, more insidious, but I no longer paid them any attention. We could keep the shadow at bay. My mom's energy felt never-ending, a deep well of light and power that would protect me for as long as I needed. I focused on the warmth of her love, and took another deep breath, pushing out all the energy I could.

Jenus

I lay with my cheek pressed against the cold stone, surrounded by my own filth. My breathing was labored and I had started to truly wonder if I was going to survive this dungeon. I hadn't quite believed that my brother would leave me down here to rot, but perhaps I had been wrong. Perhaps I had underestimated how cold and ruthless he had become.

Without a doubt, something was happening above—the ministers the guards had requested had never come, and an hour previously, the extra sentries they'd brought down to watch me had all been called above. They had syphoned me aggressively before they left, taking every ounce of my energy. Leaving me close to death.

I no longer held out hope that my master was coming. What would he want with me? I was wretched, no better than an animal, sniveling on the floor, too weak to rise.

"What's that?" one of the guards exclaimed suddenly, rising off the overturned barrel he was using as a chair. "Who goes there?" he called, swiveling around the room, then turning to look at his fellow guard with unease. No one replied.

A moment later I heard thumping from the corner of the room—something large and heavy was being dislodged. The stone floor trembled with the movement, barrels and crates being upturned.

"Announce yourself!" called the guard, unsheathing his broadsword and pointing it toward the barrels.

"Easy," said the second guard, "easy—it might just be an animal."

Both the guard and I turned to look at him with incredulous expressions.

Fool.

"That's no animal," the first guard replied angrily. "Nothing's that strong!"

The second guard armed himself too, and they waited anxiously by my cage, their eyes darting over to my still figure every other second.

I laughed to myself. What did they think I could possibly do? I was as helpless as a newborn, and unless the noise was my master himself, I was done for.

A bang rocked the room, followed by the sound of a stone sliding heavily across the floor. Someone was coming in.

The guards instantly tried to syphon off the intruder, their faces contorted with the effort. It was having little effect. A large, heavy figure moved up from the darkness, stepping out into the gloom.

Master?

The guards started to scream. They fell to the ground, twitching and gasping, their swords forgotten in their outstretched hands. I tried to pull myself up, my arms trembling with the effort.

The figure stepped out into the light. I recognized her—a village woman, one who claimed to be some kind of apothecary.

"Jenus of Hellswan," she noted with disgust, breaking the barriers that surrounded my cage with a single swipe of her hand.

"Who were you expecting?" I rasped, my mouth filling with bile at the disappointment. I had hoped I would be saved, but this woman was no friend of mine.

"You don't look good," she mocked.

"I look as well as can be expected. My foul brother has chained and drained me—what's your excuse?"

She ignored my bitter comments, searching the bodies of

the guards. Her large body moved with surprisingly agile speed as she sifted through their robes.

"What are you doing?" I hissed.

"Getting the keys to your little bird cage. This castle was the original safe house for the Acolytes. That"—she pointed to the hole from which she'd just emerged—"is a safe passage that will eventually lead us back to the temple—it was built centuries ago, and forgotten. Till now."

The Acolytes.

Perhaps I was saved after all.

"For some reason," the woman continued, "my master wishes you free, and so I am here doing his duty. Despite my personal feelings toward you."

"I don't care about your personal feelings." I coughed, hacking up blood-tinged phlegm. "But I can't walk out of here. You'll have to let me syphon off you."

"Absolutely not," she retorted, jangling the keys in the palm of her hand. "Ah, here it is."

She bent down toward the lock, her ginormous behind protruding into the air as she fiddled with the key.

"If you're a servant of the master, then you are a servant of mine!" I started to syphon off her, but I was too weak. She laughed, returning the favor. I squealed, falling back onto the stone floor.

"Control yourself," she snapped. "As soon as they realize the shadow is a diversion, they'll come to check on you. We are running out of time as it is."

She unlocked the door, letting it swing open, but then returned to the hole in the floor, waiting by it expectantly, her irritation evident.

"I was being honest," I whimpered. "I can't move. You will have to carry me."

"Get *up!*" she said.

"Where is our master?" I cried, hating this wretched woman who he had sent in his place. All the Acolytes I had known had been of some standing—ministers, lieutenants and commanders—not simple-minded medicine women. "Why did he send *you?*"

"If you don't stop complaining I will leave you here, no matter what the master says. I will happily take your place!"

At her threat, I struggled onto my elbows, then grabbed hold of the bars, using them to pull my limp body into a standing position.

"Fortunately for you, the tunnel is small—you can crawl most of the way."

I gritted my teeth, unable to speak.

"Come on! Our master waits most impatiently! Every moment you spend in here you delay his plans and our day of glory!"

My day of glory.

My bones feeling like rubber, I stumbled toward her. The room spun, my own sweat falling down onto my lips with the effort.

"You smell entirely foul," she added, gagging. I reached out, using her podgy arm for support, but she shook me off.

"*Crawl*," she spat.

I nodded, staring down into the black hole, just large enough for me to enter. If I'd had the energy, I would have laughed. I had absolutely no idea how she had managed to crawl through it in the first place.

"Now!" she screamed. "They'll know where we've gone. We have to hurry, or they'll chase us down in the tunnel!"

"I…am…moving," I exhaled, sliding my body further down into the dirt.

"The shadows will give us cover at the cove," she added, heaving her body into the hole, legs first. "Just pray that we get there in time—your brother has been joined by a supernatural fighting force of some kind. We can't be too careful."

A supernatural fighting force?

Perhaps the woman was truly as mad as she looked. A heavy clunk sounded as the stone was replaced, and we were submerged in complete darkness.

DEREK

I was starting to feel a similar sensation to the one I had experienced when the woman from the tower drained us of energy—the gray dots dancing about my vision, and the light-headed, woozy effect which indicated I was on my way to losing consciousness. The only difference was, it never happened. The sentry syphoning off me, a robed minister who had attended the meeting, seemed to maintain a precarious balance of his energy supply—never draining me too much, keeping his supply constant. Begrudgingly, I had to admit that it was impressive.

"Derek, you okay?" Lucas asked me.

"Fine. You?"

My brother nodded. He was standing next to me, providing his services to another minister. Everywhere I looked I could see members of GASP standing stone-still, running down like batteries. Only the witches managed to stay strong, using their own innate power to uphold the barriers. For the rest of us, there hadn't been time to ask where or how we would replenish our energy supplies, but it would have to be done swiftly if our efforts to repel the shadow worked.

Suddenly, a shout went up.

"It's withdrawing!"

I looked up, the shadow having worked itself almost completely over the bubble of protection that the barriers had provided. Now I could see it drawing back. Slowly, inch by inch, the impenetrable blackness of the shadow was being replaced by the lighter tones of the evening sky.

"It worked," exhaled the minister in front of me.

"I thought our time might have come," Lucas muttered grimly.

I knew what he meant—the ice that had grasped at my heart was like nothing I'd ever felt. There might not have been anything *physical* to fight, but I had felt like this evil could kill me from the inside—crushing my brain and senses till there was nothing left but the madness of a broken mind.

Why hadn't it?

What I had felt, the power that had come from that shadow,

could have ended us, I was sure of it. We had maintained the barriers, but for how long would we have been able to do so? Our strategy had been to repel, not to attack. We were weak—without weapons that could fight the shadow effectively, why had it not continued to remain, waiting till we had exhausted our energy supplies?

The shadow vanished, the whispering dying off to be replaced with the gentle rustling of the trees in the wind.

"Uh, brother?" Lucas prompted.

"What?" I snapped, irritated to have my chain of thought broken. Lucas gestured to the approaching figure of Tejus, making his way through the GASP members and sentries who had sat down on the ground, resting.

I had seen my granddaughter working the sentry magic along with the others. Clearly, this was what Kira had warned me about. It pained me to see what she had become. I still didn't know enough about their kind to truly understand why she would have wanted to do such a thing—most likely it was the sway of her boyfriend. Had infatuation blinded her? Or had she chosen this life with a level head… all for this man? My only fear was that she'd had no choice in it at all—perhaps not because of Tejus, even I could see that he cared deeply for her, but by some other sentry. But it didn't feel like my place to ask. Her mother would untangle the story eventually, and what needed to be done would be done. The only reassuring aspect was how comfortable Hazel had seemed in her own skin—not just as she created the barriers, but from the moment we had found her in the forest. She *had* transformed, in more ways than one, and perhaps this new life was one she embraced wholeheartedly.

"Tejus," I acknowledged with a nod of my head. For now, I would give him the benefit of the doubt. Ash was behind him, looking as weary as I felt.

"There's something about this that doesn't make sense," Tejus muttered, looking around at the empty night sky.

"I know. I can't help but think we're missing something…what was the point of that? Why has it just vanished?"

"We were winning?" Lucas replied.

I shook my head.

"No, we were surviving. We were not winning."

Silence descended on the group—Lucas looking confused, Ash and Tejus both appearing frustrated.

"A *distraction*," Tejus growled suddenly.

He was right. It was the only strategy that made sense.

But for what?

Ash groaned out loud.

"Follow me," Tejus barked, hurrying back to the castle.

He raced along the hallways, Ash, Lucas and I in close pursuit. He entered one of the rooms, revealing a sentry guard, passed out cold on the floor.

"JENUS!" Tejus bellowed, heaving back a trap door set in the stone floor. He disappeared from view, and after a few seconds, we followed him. We entered a dank basement, where two more guards lay on the floor. In the center of the room there was a cage—almost like a large bird cage, inch thick in filth.

"That *parasite*!" Tejus swore.

"Who?" I demanded, turning to Ash, hoping I could get some actual answers out of him.

"Tejus's brother. They don't get along."

I exchanged a glance with Lucas, who grimaced.

That sounded familiar.

"Do you think he's in league with the Acolytes? Do you think any of them were left alive, to help him?" Ash asked Tejus.

"I can't see how we'd think otherwise." Tejus sighed. "I think he escaped here."

Tejus pointed to one of the floor stones. It was in place, but the barrels and other items that covered most of the floor and walls had been moved away from it.

"Someone must have come in this way too," he continued, moving the stone back from the floor. It revealed a hole in the ground—small, but large enough for someone to crawl through. I cursed them for not checking the room properly. It should have been completely secured.

"He wouldn't have been able to do this on his own. He was too weak," Tejus muttered.

"Why weren't we told of a prisoner down in the dungeons?" I asked.

"We didn't think he posed that much of a threat. Queen Trina was dead, as were the rest of the Acolytes. We assumed. I didn't imagine for a moment that the entity would have much use for him." Tejus's reply was furious, and I knew from my own experience that the anger was directed inward.

Ash muttered something about 'pride before a fall' and Tejus silenced him with a stony glare.

"Do we go after him?" Lucas asked.

"Would there be any point?" I asked the sentries.

"The stone is marked with the old Acolyte rune," Ash replied, looking closely at the slab. "It probably leads back down to the cove—they have a temple there. I don't think we should risk it. Not now, anyway."

"All right," I agreed. "Move the stone back. Is there a seal you can put on it?"

"We can put a barrier in place." Ash nodded. "I'll get the ministers on it. In the meantime, we need to try to understand what the entity wants with Jenus—I thought it was too powerful to want another servant. What can Jenus do for it that it can't do for itself?"

That was the question. If Tejus was right, and his brother was indeed weak, then what would this power want with him? And who had rescued him in the first place?

We made our way back up the stairs. When we entered the hallway, Ben, River, Sofia, Rose, Caleb, Hazel, Ruby, Grace and Lawrence were waiting for us.

"What happened?" Hazel asked. "Has he gone?"

I filled in the other members on the situation with Tejus's brother.

Hazel was the first to offer her theory.

"It must have been Abelle. She's the only Acolyte alive—"

"That we know of," Ash interrupted. "And she hated Jenus. I know most of what she said was a lie, but I'd swear on my life that wasn't."

"Don't defend her," Tejus snapped. "If she is in league with the entity then she's going to be willing to do what it wants. Even if that means pulling my loathsome brother from his sewer."

"Let's go over the facts," I asserted, trying to bring some calm to a debate I could see was about to become heated. "This entity has escaped from the lock that the jinn placed it in. It has raised an army, so we can presume that it's grown in strength. Yet it has not faced us. I agree with Tejus, I don't believe that the shadow is the entity itself. If it were, I believe it would speak to us just like it did in the portal. So why has it not fully risen—what is missing?"

"Queen Trina," whispered Hazel. "He used her from the start, he must have wanted something from her—maybe something more than just opening the portal."

I nodded. She was the missing piece. Killing her was the only time that the sentries had been one step ahead.

I thought about the entity and its prison of stones.

A non-corporeal being.

"It reminds me of the Elders," I muttered. "They didn't have physical form and so took other bodies. I have, mistakenly perhaps, been assuming that the shadow is an effective weapon—but perhaps its army *can't* take on physical form, and neither can the entity itself."

"Which is what it needed Queen Trina for, but its only option now is my brother," Tejus said.

"And Benedict," Hazel agreed. "Throughout all of this the entity has needed bodies to accomplish what it can't."

"But what does it need a body for?" Grace asked quietly. "It has an army, the portal is opened, what is it waiting for?"

"That is what we don't know," I replied.

"Shouldn't we try to stop Jenus from getting to the entity then?" Lucas snapped. "Why are we just standing around doing nothing, waiting for it to come to us?"

"We can't risk another trip to the cove, not without the right weapons," Ash replied. "I won't let my people risk their lives like that."

"And GASP can't, we're too weak," I reminded Lucas. "It would be a mistake. How do we heal?" I asked Ash.

"Your energy rebuilds itself. Unfortunately, you just need to wait it out."

I looked from Hazel to Ruby incredulously. This was madness. We didn't have the time for bed rest.

"What about your crystals, Tejus?" Hazel asked. "Are there more of those around Nevertide? They helped me during the trials." My granddaughter looked uncomfortable for a moment.

"There are," Tejus replied, "but far away from here. We'd have to cross the northern forests – and even then it would take me days to fill the stones with my energy."

"No way," interjected Ash. "No forests. I'm sticking by what I said earlier. The entity's army seems stronger there. We should stick to open land. It's too risky."

"So we just have to wait?" Lucas exclaimed.

"Wait," Ruby replied suddenly, "what about the water—it has rejuvenation properties, right? We're going there anyway, but it can heal GASP and the rest of us too. Maybe we can even take the kids. We might need to use them for syphoning again."

Sofia shuddered at the mention of the children who had been kidnapped—used and abused too much by the sentries already.

"No," my wife interjected. "They've been through enough. I want to leave them out of this."

Ruby nodded in understanding, looking a little shamefaced. I took pity on her. We all knew what it was like fighting for our lives against impossible odds—we used what tools we could in the moment, hoping that the consequences weren't too severe.

"You've protected them from danger long enough." I spoke to Ruby directly. "We can't worry about them during a battle. The sentries can use GASP—we should provide more than enough energy once it's replenished."

"Then what are we waiting for?" Lucas said. "Let's go."

Tejus looked at Ash, who nodded.

It was time.

SHERUS

It was still nightfall when we rode out. We were all weak, tired and depleted by the magic of these strange creatures. The dragons and the Hawks flew ahead, scanning the land for danger…but how would they spot a shadow? I didn't agree with Derek's decision to ride at nightfall—especially not on these deformed bull-horses, which seemed horrifically unnatural to me. I chose to float along beside my sister, who had also chosen to ride. Some of the sentries rode on large vultures, and some joined our ranks on foot. Few spoke, and we mostly peered into the darkness that surrounded us, waiting for the whispering to begin.

Ghouls' Ridge was where we were headed—what good

could come of a place with that name?

"Peace, Sherus," Lidera murmured softly. "I can see your mind spinning. These waters sound like our only hope."

"We should have traveled in the daylight," I grunted.

"We're exposed either way. I agree with King Derek—better to travel as soon as possible."

I ignored my sister. She tended to agree with anyone who wasn't me. I couldn't help but think the whole mission was a disaster. The portal was still open—those wretched creatures could get out at any time, floating onward into the In-Between and destroying my kin. Why had we not just closed it and left these sentries to their fate? Their own emperor had been foolish enough to release it in the first place—perhaps it was right that they should pay for their mistakes.

Like you did?

I sighed heavily. Benjamin. He had been the reason I hadn't faced the consequences of my own father's deal with the ghouls. I owed Derek and his kin this much.

The vampire king rode up to me, letting the others ride ahead as his bull-horse fell into step alongside me.

"We need to understand exactly what the entity wants," Derek said. "More specifically, why he might seek to destroy the In-Between once he has finished in this dimension."

"I have been wondering that myself, but I haven't come to any valid conclusions. If I knew what kind of creature this entity actually was, perhaps I would understand more. But no one seems to be able to tell us," I grumbled.

"Go easy on them, Sherus," Derek reprimanded me. "They are mere children compared to you, and you have failed in learning the history of the stones… You are just as much at fault here."

I grunted my agreement, not willing to wholeheartedly own up to my part in this. But he was right. I had known about the land watched over by the Shadowed fae, but never questioned what they guarded. I should have been more vigilant.

"I am worried about my ability to protect my people from this danger." I sighed.

"We may overcome them here. Can you sense if any have gotten out and into the In-Between?"

I shook my head. "I believe that I would know—and so far, I feel we are safe. But that is my instinct only, it may not be fact."

"You have not doubted your instincts up till now, Sherus. Don't start now. Let's have hope that we can win this battle."

We continued on in silence. I watched the stars above— both those of this sky, and those twinkling in the abyss exposed by the rip. To fae, the sky was precious, beloved for all its colors and temperament—the closest our kind came to worship. We read its signs, it told us histories and stories through the configuration of its stars. The degradation of this sky seemed utterly barbaric to me, an act so sinful that it made me shudder every time I looked upon it. What destruction would this creature wreak on my home?

"Derek," my sister interrupted, "I hear your granddaughter is one of these creatures… I am surprised that Tejus still lives."

Derek looked straight ahead, his jaw clenching. He chose not to answer my sister and I didn't blame him. It should be the least of his concerns right now—yet, if it had been one of my own, I wondered how I would have felt.

"He is a supernatural creature," Derek replied eventually. "And an apparently honorable one, who knows how to command an army, and obviously cares deeply for my granddaughter. I am tired of raging against the men the women in this family choose, only to be proven wrong." He smirked, perhaps thinking of his son-in-law. "Hazel, I think, can handle him."

"We fae are less keen on interbreeding, perhaps wrongly," my sister commented. "Wouldn't you say, Sherus?"

I shrugged. It was no matter to me.

"I, uh, believe a certain almond-eyed jinni queen has caught my brother's attention," whispered Lidera to Derek.

"*Silence*, Lidera!" I barked.

I sighed once again as the heat rose in my cheeks—I was deeply regretting bringing my irritating kin along.

Ruby

Soon we were approaching Ghouls' Ridge, our journey uneventful except for the argument between Hazel and her mom, which Benedict seemed determined to make worse. I rode between Ash and Tejus, feeling utterly awkward as every word exchanged floated across to us.

"Do you think I should say something?" I asked Ash quietly.

"No." He laughed.

"It's not that funny unless you want to be having the same argument with my mom, which, by the way, as soon as word gets out on the…*logistics* of it, you will!"

He fell silent.

"Maybe you should say something," he murmured after a

while.

"You'll make it worse," Tejus snapped.

I really felt for the guy. It couldn't be easy suddenly being confronted with the whole of Hazel's family when I knew he'd only just started to forgive himself for what had happened.

"You know Hazel loves her sentry powers, right?" I said.

He looked at me sidelong in surprise. "It's been difficult for her—constantly feeling the need to feed," he corrected me.

"I know that, but it would hardly be much different if she was a vampire. She gets that now—I think she was just shocked in the beginning. She was pretty sold on becoming a vampire. Trust me, if she hasn't told you already, she does enjoy them. She's different. More confident. It's nice to see."

Tejus didn't comment again, but I could see him mulling over the information I'd just given him. I could only hope that when the time came, I would embrace my powers the way Hazel had—welcoming them, strengthening them so that I could be of use to my family and the rest of GASP.

I'd seen how impressed Grace, Arwen and the others had been when Hazel had joined the rest of the sentries in upholding the barriers. True Sight, syphoning, impenetrable barriers—they were all going to be helpful in the fight to protect the human and supernatural worlds.

I smiled at Ash, running my fingers across the golden band around my finger. I still hadn't told Hazel. I couldn't wait to share the news with her.

"We're here," Tejus announced.

I looked up the huge cliff face. At night-time, it looked even more eerie than it did in the day, the mists blanketing the night sky so we could hardly see a thing. I thought about the rest of the Impartial Ministers floating in the water like dead bodies in a lake. I shuddered. At least it would be light in the cave.

"Not looking forward to finding the entrance in the dark," Ash muttered.

"We should send the vamps first—amazing night vision."

"Oh, really?"

I nodded, laughing at his look of amazement. If he was impressed now, I couldn't wait till he saw them fight. I kept forgetting that Ash had no experience with vamps, werewolves, dragons and Hawks—it was so strange to me now to come across someone who wasn't aware of our kind.

My mom, Rose and Derek approached us.

"What now?" Derek asked.

"There's an entrance where the cliff meets the valley walls, over there." Ash pointed in the direction of the slit in the rocks. "You might be able to navigate it better."

Derek nodded, immediately seeing the entranceway. I looked back at the team with us. All of GASP had come along, and most of the ministers—the rest of the kids, villagers and guards had stayed behind, maintaining the barriers. Still, it meant that our group was easily over one hundred.

Ash followed my glance.

"We should leave the sentries out here to guard. GASP and the rest of us go in," Ash said.

Derek nodded. "Are we expecting danger inside?"

"No," Tejus replied, "it should only be the Impartial Ministers in there, if anyone—but we can't be too careful."

Derek and Sofia were the first to enter the passage, with Ash, Tejus, Hazel and me following. I doubted that Derek would be as amazed as we were the first time he saw the ministerial home, he'd seen a lot in his time, but when he approached the blazing light and stepped through to the miraculous open-air chamber, the vampire stopped still.

He turned to me and Hazel.

"We need Ibrahim. The light in here is bright."

We fetched Ibrahim, asking the rest to stand back in the valley while the warlock worked his magic. A few moments later we were given the all clear, and the rest of GASP entered the large chamber.

Ash, Tejus, Hazel and I strode over to the water, looking down into its white waters.

"Where are they?" I asked. The waters were empty; the bodies of the Impartial Ministers had vanished. The rest of us looked as puzzled as I did—I didn't know why they'd leave, the whole point of the water was to restore them.

"Did we bring the Impartial Ministers?" Ash asked.

"We did." Tejus nodded, walking back toward the group. A few moments later he reappeared, with both of the Impartial Ministers following behind him.

"This is sacrilege!" one of them chastised him, banging his walking staff on the polished marble floor so it echoed loudly around the room. Tejus rolled his eyes, leading them up to the edge of the basin.

"Where are they?" he asked bluntly.

Both ministers peered down into the water, shaking their heads in sorrow.

"Perhaps they went to hide—to find a safe haven far from the dangers of this land. Far from *you*, Tejus of Hellswan!"

"Didn't they need the water?" I asked.

"They did," the minister grunted. "And probably won't last long without it. The same as us. You may well be trying to destroy the entity with this foolhardy effort, but you will end us—the guardians of the very land you're trying to save!"

I glanced over at Tejus and Ash. I knew the Impartial Ministers weren't even close to being a priority right now, but I felt bad for the men. I knew they'd been stupid—arrogant and blind-sided by rules and propriety, but still, they had only been doing what they thought was best, and perhaps they deserved some compassion.

"What's Derek going to do with the water?" Ash asked,

completely ignoring the minister.

"I don't know yet," I replied. "But maybe we can save some…for them?"

I looked over at the Impartial Ministers, who scowled at me. *Never mind.*

"We'll see," Tejus replied.

After admiring the massive chambers, the members of GASP were making their way over to where we stood. Derek walked with Ibrahim, Mona and Corrine, all in deep discussion. When they approached the basin, Ibrahim placed his hands above the surface of the water and closed his eyes.

"It's powerful," he murmured.

At the opposite end of the pool, Sherus and Nuriya bent down to get a closer look. Sherus placed a finger in the water, gently rippling its surface.

"These are the waters of *immortalitatem*," he confirmed. "See the eternal light? It continues to blaze brightly for all time, yet the waters remain as cold as ice."

I looked down at the bottom of the pool, the pure white light glowing just the way it did in Hazel's dagger.

"What can you do, Ibrahim?" Derek asked.

The warlock considered the question for a while, staring down at the water as if working out some puzzle, his hand continuously moving over the water, testing its power. After a while, he turned back to Derek.

"I can infuse our weapons with the waters, ensuring that we each have access to the water's power. For those who don't carry material weapons, natural ones will work too."

"Fangs?" Erik asked.

Ibrahim nodded.

"Excellent," Kiev muttered.

At the warlock's request, we all stood back while the witches went to work. Mona, Corrine, Brock and Arwen stood around the pool, their hands out in the same way Ibrahim held his. Soon the water started to move, rising up to meet the tips of their fingers, the light from within shining bright and pearlescent as it was drawn up into the sunlit chamber.

"Each come forward and state your weapon of choice," Ibrahim announced.

An orderly queue stood behind the warlock: Ash, Tejus and I brandishing swords; Benedict clasping a crossbow and bolts; the dragons and Hawks requesting that their claws be cast in the water, all transforming into the supernatural state in preparation; and the vampires and werewolves, most holding weapons, but all grinning, showing their deadly sharp incisors.

Ash was first, but sidestepped and gently urged me forward to go first. I didn't think he was worried, more a gentleman, but I was looking forward to his reaction when he saw what Ibrahim could do.

I stepped up onto the edge of the basin, holding out my

sword. It was an impressive-looking piece, a light blue steel with an elaborate handle, bearing the markings of the Memenion kingdom. Ash had given it to me before we left, making sure that I would have something to protect me from the shadows.

I held it aloft, and Ibrahim muttered incomprehensible words under his breath. The water started to move toward me, a thin stream rising up in mid-air, breaking off from the pool. Slowly it began snaking itself around my sword, without touching it. Droplets started to fall on the weapon, each landing with a hiss as if the blade was burning. Soon the snake of water had disappeared entirely—the water had infused into the weapon, making it gleam brightly.

"Wow," I whispered.

Ibrahim smiled at me.

"Take care, Ruby."

"I will," I replied, staring at the blade. The handle felt warmer than it had before the infusion, but that could have just been from holding it—and I could have sworn I could actually see the bright light glowing through the steel.

I stepped back down, letting Ash take his turn. He looked a little paler than usual. When Ibrahim had finished, working his magic on the sword of Hellswan, he joined me.

"How was that?" I prompted.

Ash was silent for a few moments.

"*Amazing,*" he said, still looking a little out of sorts.

"You'll get used to it eventually," I replied, taking his hand. "I guess in the same way I've gotten used to the sentry stuff you can do."

He nodded, looking over at the jinn who were standing back from the basin, watching the rest of us.

"What about the jinn?" he asked.

"They'll probably rely on their own magic. Technically, the waters were supposedly created by them in the first place."

Queen Nuriya whispered something to Aisha. The younger jinni left the room with her husband, returning later with some small water flasks they must have taken from the saddles. Then Aisha and Horatio joined the back of the line.

"Aisha, what are you going to do with the water?" I asked.

"We will do our own thing, infusing it into our bodies and our magic. But we don't trust a warlock to do it. No disrespect to Ibrahim, he is talented, but we must do it ourselves."

I nodded, noticing the dragons in the line whispering amongst themselves. No doubt they had their own reservations about this—they never took assistance from the witches if they could help it, at least when it came to travel.

"We should make sure the other sentries and guards all have their weapons spelled as well, right?" I asked, turning to Ash.

"We have a few barrels with us, we'll fill them and take them back to the palace."

"Should we take it all?"

"We need to take what we can," Ash replied, glancing at the Impartial Ministers sitting on the bottom of the steps that led up to the basin, muttering to one another.

"What about them?" I asked.

"We don't have a choice, Ruby. If it's between saving the rest of Nevertide's citizens and keeping a few angry old men alive, I have to choose the former. I need to see the bigger picture, and I want a fresh start for Nevertide once this is over. No trials, no entity, no Impartial Ministers deciding the outcome for the rest of us."

"Okay," I whispered.

"You'll see." He smiled, squeezing my hand. "You'll see."

ASH

"Meet me downstairs in a few hours." Tejus turned to me the moment we re-entered the barriers surrounding the palace. The witches had 'vanished' us here from Ghoul's Ridge on the return journey, now they knew the route, and the dragons had flown. I'd been dubious about being influenced by that kind of magic – I could hardly comprehend it, but I couldn't deny how convenient it was to be instantly transported.

"We need to decide the best strategy for attack," Tejus continued. "We should involve GASP as well."

"Don't you think it's best if we let the entity come to us? We can better protect ourselves here than out in the open, especially if you're thinking of going down to the cove."

"Perhaps," he mused, looking at the barriers—still holding strong after the visit from the shadow.

"Ash?"

Ruby's mother called my name. She was standing on the terrace that surrounded the entrance to the palace, along with her husband. The rest of the army were returning indoors, the warlock and witches remaining outside to infuse the weapons of the guards who had remained here.

"Damn," I breathed.

"Good luck." Tejus smirked. I didn't know what he was looking so superior about. I had absolutely no doubt that his time would come. Hazel's parents and extended family clearly knew what had happened. If Tejus thought he'd be getting away with that, then he had another thing coming.

I left Tejus, making my way to Claudia and Yuri. Dawn was coming, and the vampires seemed more deadly than usual—both lit by the red light of the sky, looking like demonic versions of my judge, jury and executioner.

"How can I help?" I asked, clearing my throat a couple of times before I could get the words out.

"We need to discuss Ruby," her mother replied, tense and frowning.

"Our engagement?" I prompted, hopefully.

"Among other things."

Like transforming her into a sentry?

I really didn't want to have this conversation right now. I still didn't know Ruby's thoughts on the matter—not fully anyway. What she'd been saying to Tejus earlier had given me hope that she might even welcome it, but I doubted her family would feel the same way. Though I didn't really understand why. The more I observed, the less difference I saw between their kind and ours.

"I know you have feelings for our daughter," Claudia continued. "But I'm worried that you're going to ask too much of her. Have you thought about the future at all? What will happen if we all survive this, and Ruby sees her friends and family returning back to our dimension, and yet you want her to stay here?" She stared at me, her brown eyes cold and calculating.

"We haven't discussed it yet," I replied. "I don't know what Ruby will want to do. I don't know what *I'll* want to do yet."

That was a lie, and Claudia knew it. If Nevertide made it through this, I wouldn't abandon my people. I couldn't.

"My daughter doesn't belong in a place like this," she snapped. "Since she was little she's wanted to become a member of GASP. I don't see how all that could have changed."

I was starting to lose my temper.

"Maybe you should be speaking to Ruby about this," I snapped.

Big mistake.

Claudia's eyes burnt through me like coals, her fangs

protruding.

"Claudia," Yuri murmured, reaching out to clasp his wife by the arm. She scoffed, looking up at me, both our tempers sparking.

"Ash, we want you to give this some thought," Yuri said. "Think about the kind of future that Ruby would have here—away from everyone she knows and loves. We're concerned about our daughter, and we just want to make sure that you've both thought this through. Ruby can be…impulsive," he added, glancing over at his wife. "I just want to be sure the two of you aren't running headlong into something that will end up making both of you miserable."

I nodded, swallowing. Yuri's more measured explanation of their concerns made me feel terrible. He was right, we hadn't given this much thought. But I also knew that we felt the same way about one another—and wasn't love supposed to conquer all? Wouldn't there be a way to work this out, as long as we did it together?

"I understand," I announced. "I get your concerns—we both do. But you have to let Ruby and me work this out. I wouldn't ever do anything to hurt her."

"Not intentionally," Yuri replied softly.

"Not intentionally or otherwise!"

This conversation needed to be over. I understood where they were coming from, but in all honestly, until we'd faced our immediate danger, I didn't want to hear it.

"I'll speak to Ruby," I promised.

"Make sure you do," Claudia replied. Her face had softened marginally. I supposed she just wanted to be heard, to have their worries known. Still, I wished they'd kept this to themselves or spoken to their daughter. I obviously didn't have the answer they wanted to hear—and I wasn't going to lie to make anyone feel better.

The pair of them left, and I stood on the terrace, turning back around to see the witches still casting their magic on an assortment of weapons. I couldn't deny that their world—and the regular human world—appealed to me. But I had been right on the day that the Impartial Ministers had crowned me emperor of Nevertide. My duties were chains to this land and its people, and I didn't quite know where that left me and Ruby.

After a while, I made my way back upstairs, wanting to speak to my fiancée before I discussed tactics with Tejus.

"Hey, you," she greeted me sleepily as I came into the room. She was wrapped in a huge bathrobe, steam still escaping from the bathroom. "Let me just get dressed and I'll be with you in a moment."

"Good idea, Shortie." I smiled. "Unless you're looking to get turned into a sentry tonight?"

She made a face at me, then, laughing, vanished back into the bathroom. A few moments later she reemerged, fully dressed, her blonde hair still damp and cascading down her shoulders. It was a pleasant sight.

"Has my mom been speaking to you?" she asked archly. "I kind of had the feeling that she might. Ignore what she says—she'll come around, I promise."

"I think there might be conditions on that," I replied dryly. "Like me returning you to The Shade, and not letting you out of her sight."

She sighed, slumping down next to me on the bed.

"We're not ready to decide that yet. We don't even know what's going to happen today—how can we make plans for the future?"

"I don't know. But we should at least talk about it. We've been avoiding the topic, among others, for a while. Shouldn't we have some kind of plan?"

"We have plans," she pointed out, waving her finger in the air. "Marriage plans. Which I can't even get properly excited about thanks to all the impending doom."

I laughed out loud. That was one way to look at it.

"Look, I have an idea. Just trust me, okay?"

"Okay," she answered slowly. I could faintly hear her heart rate picking up, and I wondered if she was worried that I was going to outright ask her to live in Nevertide with me.

Not a good sign.

"I want us to mind-meld, and basically imagine where you

want to be five years from now. Just for a few moments, what we're doing, where we are—just whatever comes to mind. I'll do the same, and maybe we'll have a better idea about what we both want…"

"Without having to come out and say it?" she retorted. "Why can't we just talk about it later?"

"Because we've been saying that for a while, Shortie—and we haven't. So just trust me on this."

She inhaled a deep breath, and then exhaled, letting her body relax.

"Okay, let's do this."

She reached for my hand, closing her small one around it. Her skin felt warm and soft, and she edged closer to me on the bed till our arms were brushing up against one another.

I closed my eyes, focusing on the energy that she was sending out toward me. In my mind, I saw it as semi-clear and fluid, almost white. *Honesty.* She wanted to be honest. I grasped onto it, sending my energy back to meet hers. For a few moments, nothing happened—we were both so exhausted I'd wondered if this was going to work at all, but after a few moments, images started to form. She was going first.

I saw bright sunshine, a house—old, pretty, built of stone, surrounded by a huge garden—filled to bursting point with flowers and unfamiliar fruit trees. I started walking toward the front door when Ruby appeared in the doorway. She smiled broadly. "Come on, you two!" she called out.

Us two? I looked down. I was holding on to the hand of a small boy, who looked up at me with bright blue eyes. He tugged, impatient. I was moving too slowly. I looked back up at Ruby. She turned away, ready to go back indoors. Her stomach protruded—another one. I followed her inside the house, overcome by the smell of more fresh flowers, and cooking.

On my right was a large living room full of furniture that seemed strange to me. Sitting on a sofa was Jenney. She was speaking into a screen, her voice serious, a small frown on her forehead. When she noticed me she smiled and waved. "I'm talking to Derek—Ruby will debrief you." She turned back to the screen, and I made my way into another room.

Ruby was standing at a stove, humming as she threw herbs into a pot. It smelled good. The boy ran toward her, wrapping himself around her leg.

"We have company," she noted, turning to me. "Tejus and Hazel."

How does she know?

Moments later there was a knock on the door.

True Sight. Ruby was a sentry. A gifted one at that. I heard the voices of our friends floating in from the hallway, but before they appeared the image started to flicker and blur. The vision was ending.

No!

I wanted to hold on to it. To me, it seemed like paradise. One I'd never even had the capacity to contemplate. I realized in that moment that my future expectations were sadly lacking. I had known only servitude in a gray, stone castle in a land where light was dull, the life for all—master or servant—harsh.

I broke the mind meld.

"What?" exclaimed Ruby. "That's not fair. You said—"

"I know what I said," I replied hoarsely. "Forget what I said. I want *that*—I want what you showed me. More than I've ever wanted anything in my life. I would give anything, Ruby— anything."

I meant it.

"Oh, Ash." She half laughed and half looked like she was about to cry. I guessed she had been as invested in that vision as I was. I couldn't get the image of our son out of my head. And Jenney—safe, happy, part of my family. "I still don't know where we were. I couldn't decide!"

"It doesn't matter," I said simply. "You were right. It doesn't matter where we are. If I get to wake up to you every morning, I'm sold."

"Softie." She nudged, poking me in the rib.

"Shortie," I retorted, gently pulling on her damp hair.

HAZEL

Tejus was pacing up and down the terrace that bordered the back of the castle. Earlier I'd tried to go to our room and get some sleep, but I was too anxious, too worried about what was to come. I'd found Tejus here, and, not knowing what else to do, had sat down, watching him walk back and forth while I tried to collect my thoughts.

His muscles were strained, each step he took seemed to have a kind of repressed aggression about it—as if he was already desperate to be on the battlefield.

"Tejus, are you okay?" I asked pointlessly. He clearly wasn't.

He turned toward me, surprised, as if he'd only just realized I was there. With a sigh, he raked his hair back from his forehead and came to sit next to me on the stone steps that led to the gardens. His elbows came to rest on his knees.

"I keep thinking that we're missing something," he replied, rubbing his unshaven jaw with his thumb. "That there's something we're not understanding. Like the fae, Sherus, saying that he had omens about the entity...why was someone from another dimension having omens about Nevertide? It doesn't make sense to me. Is this creature hoping that it will destroy this dimension and move onto the next?" He rubbed his forehead in irritation. "What makes it so sure that its plan will succeed? It makes me nervous that its rise has been so gradual, as if it's an elaborate game of chess, each of us being positioned exactly where it wants till the time is right."

I knew exactly what he meant. When GASP had told us about how they entered the portal, I recalled Benedict throwing the stone into the sea. The entity had obviously seen them there, trying to use their powers to re-open it, and, when that failed, had used the children. The same with us in the castle, before Benedict became possessed. How long had it been watching, waiting for the right kid to come along that it could use? How long had it waited for the emperor to release the stone?

"We're doing what we can," I mumbled eventually, knowing that my reassurance meant next to nothing. I shared Tejus's unspoken feeling—that we were well and truly out of our depth here.

"What does Ash say?" I asked.

He smirked, glancing at me out of the corner of his eye.

"He's too busy being given an inquisition by Ruby's parents."

"Oh," I replied sheepishly, looking down at the ground as I felt heat rise in my cheeks. I had a feeling my parents were going to be just as hard on Tejus—and the grilling my mom had given me earlier hadn't been fun.

"Just so you know, my grandfather met my grandmother when she'd been kidnapped from Earth for his harem, and my mom met my dad after *she'd* been kidnapped by vampires, my father being one of them. So, if *any* of my family even think about giving you a hard time for that, shut them down."

Tejus started laughing.

"I'll remember that," he replied, "it's quite a record."

"Tell me about it. The women in my family obviously do captivity well."

"You do. *You* were an excellent captive—polite, subservient, amenable…"

I rolled my eyes at him and elbowed his arm sharply. I expected him to laugh, but instead he grabbed me, pulling me into his lap. His face had lost all traces of humor, and he looked down at me with dark, unreadable eyes.

"Hazel, it doesn't matter what they say. What anyone says.

Watching your family today, the supernatural fighting dynasty that is your destiny, I realized that danger would never have escaped you. I'm *glad* I kidnapped you. At least this way I can protect you for the rest of my life."

"You can't protect me from everything," I reminded him gently. "In the same way that I can't protect you either."

"I can try."

I kissed him, running my hands across his shoulder blades and up to his neck, pressing myself closer against him. Just for a moment, before the danger came again, I wanted to curl up— to let myself believe that he *could* protect me—that he could take away what was bad in this world, all the memories of my brother suffering under the entity's possession, the dying face of Queen Trina that haunted me every time I closed my eyes, and the horrible, blood-curdling shadow that crept over the forests, waiting for us. If I could stay like this for just a moment, then I could imagine that we were a million miles away from here—just two people sitting on a step, looking out over a garden, nothing in the world existing except us.

It was a nice fantasy.

But we weren't ordinary people. We were soldiers. Part of a team that happened to be the only thing that stood between the entity and Nevertide's complete destruction.

"What happens now?" I asked, breaking away from the kiss.

"We decide whether we attack at the cove, or build up a

stronghold here. We need to discuss it."

I nodded. We both rose from the steps, ready to head back into the palace.

"I hate to think of the entity having watched us all that time," I muttered as we walked to the main entrance, "lying in wait, calculating its next move."

"As do I. Which is why I think we should be going to the enemy, not waiting for it to come to us."

The idea frightened me, but I agreed—and so would my grandfather. GASP members didn't wait. They fought. Bravely, fearlessly, facing the enemy head on. Not cowering behind protective barriers and castle walls.

JENUS

I stopped wondering what time of day it was. The endless blackness of the tunnel seemed to seep into my brain. In my weakened state it felt like I'd never known what daylight was—that all I had known was the dark and the slow, steady plonks of water droplets running from the ceiling to the floor.

We crawled the entire way mostly in silence, except when the apothecary chastised me for my smell. Humiliated, wet and exhausted, I continued to crawl along the passage, hoping for a small flicker of light that would indicate we were nearing our destination.

The only thing that brought me comfort was imagining the rage and disbelief on Tejus's face when he realized that I had managed to escape him. Not only had I escaped him, but I would finally be united with my master—I would have my revenge on the humans and the rest of them. To occupy my mind, I thought of all the ways I could end the life of his newly created sentry—how I would make him watch as I tortured her, drawing out the pain, making sure that each scream and cry for mercy was forever imprinted on his mind.

That would be an appropriate vengeance for all that I had suffered at the hands of my brother.

I stopped crawling. My right hand had found a space in the wall of the passage. I could feel a slight wind coming from the opening, though the air was dank and stale.

"There's an opening, do I turn?" I asked the apothecary, feeling my way along the outline of the passage. It felt like there was another tunnel joining this one.

"No, that goes to Hellswan. Keep straight."

My home.

I felt a small pang of emotion—something close to regret or sorrow, I couldn't be entirely sure. I ignored it, continuing to heave myself along the passage in the direction of the cove. Hopefully reaching the adjoining tunnel meant that our journey would soon be at an end.

Eventually, through the gloom, I started to see light. It wasn't the daylight I'd expected, but a strange greenish glow, too bright and lurid to be natural.

"What is that?" I whispered, a strange sense of awe and reverence overcoming me. It was powerful, whatever was causing that light.

"The temple of my people," she hissed. "The fact that you've never set foot in it makes me wonder why our master wants you at all. I have spent most of my life devoted to the cause—and he wants Hellswan swine instead!"

"Why would he want someone like *you*?" I shot back. "Your bloodline is lowly and poor. I am the son of an emperor, with more power and ability than you could ever hope to obtain."

Foolish woman.

"You are no longer the son of an emperor," she reminded me cruelly, "and you are weak—so weak that you let your own brother treat you no better than a four-legged beast."

I ignored her. She knew nothing. My master recognized my true power—he would know me, know the glory within me that would shine through, if only I was given the chance.

Pushing myself forward using the last remaining vestiges of my energy, I slid, face first, down into the open. I looked up from the ground. Four stone walls surrounded me, all carved with rudimentary runes, all of them bleeding green light into the chamber. In the center of the room was an oblong-shaped box, split in half as if it had burst open from the inside—its top split in two, each lying either side of its base. Crawling toward it, I peered over the top, seeing what lay within. It was empty—

just dirt lay at the bottom—and it reeked of decay.

The apothecary squeezed out of the passage.

"We need to go above," she muttered, making her way to one of the walls. She pressed her hand against the stone wall, covering one of the runes. A moment later, part of the wall slid sideways, revealing a door—and beyond that, a sandy and muddy track which led up to the cove.

I followed her up, walking with difficulty, having to hold on to the walls and then the foliage on either side of the track. I didn't want my master to see me on my knees, helpless and weak.

As soon as I emerged from the track and faced the open cove, a strange sensation crept over me. A weight settled over my being—heavy, forceful, as if it was trying to suck the life out of my body. I froze, waves of sickness welling up inside of me while grotesque, unnatural thoughts ran through my mind.

"Can you feel it?" the apothecary whispered. "It's his power."

She fell forward onto her knees, her upper body lying prostrate on the ground in worship.

I looked around, trying to focus away from the hell erupting in my brain and *see*. My eyes lighted on the large object in front of me—a strange dome, filled with erupting lightning bolts, emerging from a circle of dead bodies which were easily recognizable as the Acolytes with their black robes and, even in death, their faces were concealed by their hoods. I saw the navy blue of Queen Trina's robe, her body squashed pitifully beneath the others.

I turned my eyes away, terrified and not wishing to dwell on the sight.

Further ahead lay the frozen sea I'd glimpsed from my chains when Tejus and his armies had annihilated the Acolytes. Behind it, emerging from over the horizon, was a dark shadow—impenetrable and dense, like thunderclouds had rolled in from the ocean.

You have come to me.

My master's voice whispered to me in the breeze.

"I have, master. Do with me what you will. Bring me to glory that I might be better able to serve you!" I cried, falling down on the ground in the manner of the apothecary.

Son of Hellswan, rise up!

Elevated, proud and renewed with a sense of energy and purpose, I rose. My master wanted me. He knew I belonged on a throne, that I was better than the wretched peasant woman beside me.

"What would you have me do, master?" I asked, opening my arms up toward the sky, feeling his awe-inspiring benevolence and love bearing down on me.

You, son of Hellswan, will be an anchor to the world of the living. A powerful half-human, gifted with the magic of my people, you will serve as my body.

"A half-human?" I asked, momentarily taken aback by my master's insult.

You know yourself not, Jenus of Hellswan. But you shall. You shall see all, as I do.

"Yes, master! Gift me with your power, so I might share in your glory!"

You will become my power. Over time, we will merge as one. One being to reign over the dimensions of the humans and the fae.

I stopped, feeling a chill run down my spine. I had thought that I would rule Nevertide—had he not promised me that all along? That I would become all-powerful?

"M-my master, I do not understand—will you not gift me with emperorship? The power to rule my kin?"

You will have power, my power—till the end of days. Child— his whispers became soothing, caressing—*have you not sworn to love me? To dedicate yourself to my rise and our rule?*

"Yes, master! Yes!" I trembled, looking down at the sand with blurred vision as my eyes grew wet with tears.

"If he will not, I shall!" the apothecary cried out.

"NO!" I screamed, kicking the prostrate woman. "I am who my master wants. I will serve him faithfully!"

Very well, son of Hellswan. Step into the dome, let me meet you. Let us be joined as one.

With a sinking sensation in the pit of my stomach, I trod

slowly across the sand. Flies buzzed around the dead bodies, and the reck of their death overpowered my senses as I moved closer. I hoped that the obvious power in the dome—the strong pillar of blinding light in its center—would call to me, reassure me. But it left me cold. Petrified and alone, I reached out to grasp the nearest body. It was cold and still like stone.

"Master! Help me!" I wept.

There was no reply.

My hands trembling, I pushed myself over the bodies and stepped into the dome. The moment I did so, my energy was restored—tenfold, a thousandfold. The feeling grew and grew, power and strength filling me to bursting point.

Elated, I moved toward the pillar of light, drawn forward by the power of my master.

The moment I stepped into it, the feeling changed.

"NO!" I screamed, the cry erupting from my body, so pained and awful, it sounded like the cry of a beast, not a man.

My body felt as if it was being ripped and torn from the inside, the pain unbearable, more than I could stand. The shaft of light filled my open mouth, its power consuming me, sucking out my very soul till it felt like I was no more.

ROSE

We had decided on a course of action. The armies of Nevertide and GASP would march down to the cove in full force. Hopefully we would be taking the entity by surprise—armed with weapons infused with the waters of *immortalitatem*, which we believed would give us enough power to take down the shadows and the entity itself.

Many had misgivings about our plan. Ash and a few of the ministers of the various kingdoms had questioned the wisdom of bringing our people out into the open, with no barriers to hold back the force of the shadows. I understood their misgivings, but I knew Tejus was right. We couldn't wait. Every moment that we hung back, the opportunity of the entity to rise to its full power and escape the portal that led to the human dimension and then on to the In-Between grew greater.

"Rose, prepare the human children," my father said, stopping on his way out of the banquet room where we'd just finished the meeting. "The sentries will need to build a barrier to protect them while we're gone."

"How many sentries do we leave behind?"

"Tejus says four."

"And our children?" I asked quietly. I knew that Benedict, Julian, Ruby and Hazel would want to come along, and in truth, Hazel's powers qualified her to take part, but I was afraid for them.

"They fight with us. Tejus and Ash won't leave them. And in all honesty, I think we are better off having them with us—despite the danger. They have shown themselves to be equal to the task."

I nodded, my gut twisting.

Tejus and Hazel emerged from the hall behind him, and I left my father to get on with his preparations.

"Tejus, can I have a word with you?" I asked the sentry.

"Of course," he replied, politely.

Hazel shot me a warning glare, but left us alone.

"There was actually something I wanted to discuss with you," he said. My eyebrows shot up in surprise, but I waited for him to continue.

"I gather from what Queen Nuriya says that the jinni or jinn responsible for sealing the entity may still be somewhere in Nevertide. We are investing a lot of hope in the idea that the immortal waters will end the shadow and the entity, and I want us to have an alternate plan in case this doesn't work."

"Go on," I replied slowly.

"I thought that perhaps Benedict, Julian and your son's red-headed friend—"

"Yelena," I corrected.

"Yes—Yelena. Maybe the search for the jinn should be left to them. The shadow and the entity will be distracted; they could go about their search relatively unnoticed—there are few sentries left in the kingdoms, and fewer still who would seek to harm them." He hesitated, clearly uncomfortable with what he had to say. "I thought, now you're here, I should check with you before I gave the order."

I glanced over at my daughter, talking to Grace and Benedict by the staircase. His plan was a good one, and I was relieved that at least one of my children wouldn't be going into battle. Tejus had just risen in my estimation.

"Thank you," I replied. "I think it's a good plan. But I think they should be accompanied by one of the dragons or Hawks—and perhaps a jinni or two if we can spare them."

He nodded. "I'll speak to Derek and Ash."

When he turned on his heel to walk away, I placed my hand on his elbow, stopping him. He turned back to me with a puzzled frown.

"My daughter and son survived a very hostile land," I said, choosing my words carefully. "I'm starting to understand that you might well be a large part of the reason that they're all in one piece—and happy."

He smiled, briefly.

"Your children are impressively robust. They kept themselves alive."

I smiled back at him, knowing that he was being modest but appreciating his words all the same. My children *were* robust, but he had continually protected them, putting their lives before his own. No matter what had taken place between Tejus and my daughter, and the part he had to play in their initial kidnapping, I would forever be grateful to him for that.

I watched him walk off toward Hazel. She looked up at him worriedly, wondering what I'd said to him. He laughed and shook his head, murmuring that it was about Benedict and nothing to concern herself with. He kissed Hazel on the top of her head, and she leaned against him. She must have been tired.

"Rose?" Caleb came to stand next to me, watching the couple.

"I've changed my mind about him," I muttered.

"That was quick."

I rolled my eyes. "He loves her, clearly. What else is there to do? Keep holding a grudge against him, telling her she can't see him? She wouldn't listen and we'd lose her forever."

"I know," he murmured, "and you know that's not what I'm suggesting. It... It just feels like she's... growing up too fast!" He exhaled a breath, running a hand through his hair in exasperation. "*Way* too fast."

I looked into his brown eyes with a wide grin, wondering if he had forgotten that it hadn't been all that long ago when he had been in Tejus's shoes—under the scrutiny of my father.

He seemed to catch on to my train of thought as he cracked a small, reluctant smile. "I know... I'm finally showing my years."

Chuckling, I stood on my tiptoes and kissed his cheek. "She'll always be your little girl," I whispered. "Just like I'll always be my dad's."

He sighed again and averted his gaze toward Hazel and Tejus, a sense of brokenness still suffused in his expression. "I know we were never going to be able to protect her forever," he muttered. "I suppose a part of me just hoped our children would remain in The Shade, experiencing more peace than we ever did."

I squeezed my husband's hand as I joined him in gazing at our daughter. I had hoped for the same... just like my parents had for Ben and me.

You would have thought us Novaks would have learned our lesson by now.

Hoping for normality in the life that we Shadians lived was like hoping for dryness in the rain.

Normal wasn't what we were, and it wasn't what we'd ever be.

We lived in the line of fire, and, even with all the anxiety that came with it, I knew we would never have it any other way. Caleb and I had to accept that and be proud to see our children following in our footsteps, even if it was difficult. Their lives wouldn't be easy, but they would be rewarding.

I cleared my throat, tugging gently on Caleb's sleeve, coaxing his eyes away from our daughter and back to me.

"That's enough moping for now, Mr. Achilles," I said. "Let's go and get the other human children ready."

His face was the picture of reluctance, but he nodded. "Okay, dear."

I smirked, catching his hand and leading him toward the opposite end of the hallway where the kids had been sleeping. Jenney had been watching over them—another sentry who had gone out of her way to make sure my children were well-fed and provided for. Another inhabitant of Nevertide I was grateful for.

Despite my initial reservations, it made me think that perhaps this land truly *was* worth saving.

Benedict

"I'm taking the crossbow," I said to no-one in particular. "I think it's lucky. If they actually let us join the battle this time, I'm going to kick ass."

"Well, yeah, now it's been magicked with the immortal water, of course it is," replied Julian, in the most sarcastic voice he could manage. It didn't bother me—I knew it was because he was nervous. I wasn't going to take it personally.

"Are you thinking of taking anything else besides a sword?" I asked.

"Daggers. I found them in the armory—have you been there yet? It's pretty cool."

No!

"Why didn't you tell me there was an armory?" I yelled.

Julian shrugged. "You seemed so pleased with your crossbow."

I turned away in a huff and saw Yelena sitting on the bay of a window, watching us with a scowl on her face.

"What's up with you?" I asked.

"Jenney just told me that all the humans are going to be staying behind. Again. I bet they let you go just because you've got vampire parents—it's not *fair*. It's not like you're vampires."

"Yeah, but we will be," I pointed out, "and we probably have latent fighting skills like theirs."

She scoffed, rolling her eyes in disbelief. I thought that was a possibility—how could we not be badass when we had such badass parents? Yelena's parents were probably school teachers or something. Maybe even dentists.

"What do your parents do?" I asked, wondering why Yelena had never really talked about them much.

She mumbled something I couldn't quite catch.

"What?"

"I said, they're *accountants*."

I hid a smile. I had been close.

"Don't laugh!"

"I'm not," I protested. "It's just that it's very different from my parents. That's all."

"You're such an idiot sometimes," she sighed, turning her face out to the window and ignoring me. I could see her cheeks starting to flush red, and I felt guilty. It wasn't her fault her parents had boring jobs.

"Do you miss them?" I asked.

She carried on looking out of the window, and I thought she wasn't going to reply, but after a while she did.

"Sometimes. I don't know. We never spent much time together as a family anyway. They like computers, a lot. And I'm too noisy."

"Well," I replied, feeling generous, "maybe when we get back to Earth you can come and stay in The Shade sometimes, with us. Like on vacation or something."

"Really?" Her face lit up, and she beamed at me.

"Well, yeah. Don't get too excited. I'd have to check with my mom, and all the other GASP members. We don't just let *anyone* in… but maybe if you're lucky."

My reply hadn't dampened her spirits, and she leapt off the bay.

"I think I'd make a really good fighter," she announced. "I was thinking after this I might join the army. Maybe eventually become a marine!"

"A marine? You're too young to join the army," I retorted.

"One day I will," she corrected herself. "But before that I can train at GASP headquarters. That will definitely get me in."

I turned back to my crossbow. I didn't know why she was so desperate to go to war—not that there had been any recent human wars anyway. I couldn't imagine human wars were as clear-cut as supernatural battles. At least we always knew we were helping someone.

"Is Jenney staying here with you?" Julian asked.

"I don't know." Yelena shrugged. "Maybe? I don't know how else all the kids are going to look after themselves. What if you all die? We'll be stuck here forever, wandering the castle like ghosts."

"Yelena!" I exclaimed. "Can you not say stuff like that? We're not all going to die—right, Julian?"

"We don't know that," he replied somberly.

It wasn't what I wanted to hear. Of course we weren't going to die—our parents were here! They'd never let anyone hurt us. Julian was being dramatic.

"Boys?"

My mom and grandpa peered around the door to our room.

"Hey." I waved lamely in greeting and put the crossbow down before they could yell at me for playing with weapons indoors.

They walked in, followed by Ashley. I could tell by their expressions that they had something serious to discuss—but the appearance of my grandpa threw me. What with him always saving the world and stuff, I rarely got to spend much time with him. To be honest, he kind of scared me. Julian eyed them warily, smiling weakly at his mom.

Are we in trouble?

"We've got something we want to discuss with you," my mom began. "Why don't you all sit down? Julian, do you want to put the sword away?"

He hurriedly shoved it on the bed, and we all gathered on the sofa. Yelena stayed put.

"You too, Yelena," my mom said, smiling at her.

She shoved herself between me and Julian, trying her best to look serious and attentive.

Teacher's pet.

"We know how eager you are to join us at the cove"—my mom smiled at me—"but there's another mission that needs to be taken care of. We believe the jinni who bound the entity in the stones is still somewhere in Nevertide. We need them to be found and brought forward to help us end this."

"It's imperative that they are found," my grandfather added. "Our success in this battle may well depend on it—if we fail, you'll be our only hope."

"You want us to find the jinni?" I asked, making sure I was understanding this correctly.

"You're the only ones we would trust," my grandfather confirmed. He gazed at me, his expression serious and hopeful.

"Do you think they'd be willing to help, even if we found

them? They haven't come forward—but they must know what's going on?"

"That's a good point, Benedict, but we're hoping that you'll find a way to persuade them," he replied.

I nodded, swelling with pride. I'd never been asked to go on a special mission before—and to be asked by my grandfather, Derek Novak himself, made my toes curl. I'd always been a tiny bit jealous of my uncle, Benjamin. He was a natural leader— always kept his cool, fought amazingly well and always seemed to be making big decisions with my grandpa. I hoped one day that would be me—and maybe if I did well on *this* mission, my grandpa might trust me with more.

"And me?" Yelena asked quietly. "Am I going?"

"Yes, we hoped you would," my mom replied.

What?

Clearly I'd missed that bit when they were explaining what we had to do. Why was Yelena coming? She was a civilian— what help would she be? I looked across at Julian.

Can you believe this? I asked silently, with a pointed eyebrow raise. He just shrugged, turning his attention back to the adults.

"So, get your stuff together, we'll help you pack camping equipment—we brought our packs with us, so you can take those," Ashley explained, "and you'll be joined by Ridan, Horatio and Aisha and a few of the half-Hawk brothers."

More people?

"But we'll be in charge of the mission, right?" I asked.

"*You're* in charge, Benedict." My grandpa turned to me, a small smile creeping across his lips. "The rest know that. You'll call the shots—but remember that a good leader always listens."

"I'll remember," I vowed.

"You'll march out with us," my mom told us, "and then go in the opposite direction of the cove. Tejus will tell you where he thinks you ought to head."

I nodded, glad that we'd be traveling out with the rest of the army. It would be more exciting that way—I couldn't wait to see GASP all armed to the teeth and ready for a fight.

The adults left the room soon after. As soon as the door shut, I turned to Julian in excitement.

"Our own mission!" I exclaimed, raising my hand for a high-five. Julian rolled his eyes and yanked my hand down.

"Don't you get it?" he whispered, dragging me away from Yelena, who was now busy rifling through the drawers for spare clothes to take on the trip.

"Get what?" I asked, genuinely confused. Why wasn't he happy about this? I'd thought Julian would be over the moon, like I was.

"This is like, like a *pity* mission so that we stay out of harm's way—that's why they're letting Yelena in on it!"

I frowned at him. "What do you mean? What about Horatio

and Aisha? And the Hawks? The half-Hawk brothers, Field, Blue – they're awesome. They would have needed all of them for the fight."

"To look after *us!*"

I fell silent, thinking about what Julian was saying. I knew without a doubt that finding the jinni (or jinn) was important—if it or they were still in Nevertide, which was possible, then it was worth looking for them. Yes, it would be less dangerous than going into battle, but did that matter? If the outcome was so important? I guessed more than anything Julian's pride was hurt, because I knew he'd actually prefer us to stay out of harm's way.

I looked over at Yelena, her red head buried in one of the drawers as she threw out moth-eaten blankets. I thought about her wielding a sword, fighting the black gloom that had overshadowed the palace—coming face to face with the dark power of the entity that had totally obliterated every part of what was *me* when I was under its possession.

If this was a way that Yelena didn't have to do that stuff, didn't have to be near it, then maybe that was a good enough reason to do this.

"Yeah, well, I don't care," I replied. "I think our mission's cool. And Yelena can be helpful—she's going to be in the *marines.*"

"Whatever." Julian sighed, going over to the bed to pick up

his sword.

I glanced over at Yclena to see her beaming at me.

Huh.

ASH

I paced the grounds of the palace, watching the sentry and GASP armies preparing for battle. It wasn't yet dawn, and we would be marching out before first light. The witches were making last-minute checks of swords, daggers and any other weaponry, ensuring that all equipment was infused with the immortal waters. The guards were grim-faced, the atmosphere subdued. If it had been our first battle, I imagined things would be different—but all these men had witnessed what happened at the cove. They had all seen the shadows that crawled up the barrier, all heard the whispering. No one was under any illusions about the danger we were about to face.

"Emperor." One of the guards stepped in front of me,

bowing low. "The commander requested that you take additional weaponry into battle along with the Hellswan sword."

I nodded. "Fine. Another broadsword then, and a short blade."

The guard nodded, and went to do my bidding. It was strange having other sentries do as I asked—ministers and guards. I never wanted to get used to it. I would never abuse my power, but at times like this, when my brain was throbbing from battle strategy, worry and fear, it was a relief not to have to think about the million other small things.

We would be leaving for the cove shortly, and I still felt that we were unprepared. Many were still waiting to get their weapons spelled. Tejus and Derek were still deliberating about how they would divide the armies for maximum effect. I had left the strategizing to the two of them—I knew it wasn't where my strengths lay, and that was fine with me. I was just glad I had Tejus by my side. He was a born warrior. His coldness and stoic tendencies made him an ideal commander, willing to make the hard decisions that the rest of us couldn't.

"Have you seen Ruby?" I asked Hazel as I caught her walking past, her arms piled so high with the strange black packs that GASP had brought with them, she couldn't see over them.

"I think she's in the kids' room—or she was. You want me

to send her your way if I see her?"

"Thanks, Hazel."

She walked on, narrowly avoiding tripping over one of the tent pegs.

"Use True Sight!" I yelled after her.

"Got it!" she called back. Hazel's hunger seemed to be under control, and I was glad for her. Syphoning off the vampires and other supernatural creatures certainly made a difference – their energy levels were astonishing.

I decided to look for Ruby myself, and started to walk back toward the castle. The entrance was empty—most of the ministers and guards were outside, and the rest of GASP with them. I checked the kids' room, but only saw the children, sitting around reading and playing with wooden swords, ironically. There were a few villagers around, but no Ruby. I came back out and headed upstairs to the sleeping quarters.

I found Ruby in our bedroom. Her back was to me, and she didn't turn around as I entered, too engrossed with staring at a dark, military-style outfit laid out on the bed.

"What's that?" I asked.

She jumped, evidently surprised that there was someone else in the room with her, and then relaxed when she saw who it was.

"It's a GASP uniform. My mom brought a spare in her pack. She says it will fit me."

"Have you tried it on?" I asked, wondering why she seemed so distant and thoughtful.

"No," she replied, letting out a huge sigh.

I walked over to get a closer look. The outfit didn't look too daunting to me—aside from all the blackness. Just pants, a top, boots and a belt. It looked entirely bizarre from my point of view—the material seemed weird, but I guessed this was modern stuff from her world and all the other members of GASP were wearing it.

"What's wrong with it?" I asked.

"Nothing."

"Well, something's wrong. Is it the battle?"

She looked at me directly, surprised by the question.

"No, it's not that. I guess…Well, I've been waiting for this moment all my life. I just thought I'd be better prepared for it—like, more training and stuff. The way it normally works is that the younger members start off on small cases and then work their way up. I suppose this feels like diving in at the deep end…and…I don't know! I feel like I'm not ready—I've not *earned* it, how am I going to do it justice?" she cried, her face becoming redder and redder as she made her speech.

"I heard that Benedict and the others are going to look for the jinn. If you don't feel ready, then maybe that would be a better plan?" I asked hopefully. I was having second thoughts about Ruby joining the battle—I didn't want her to endanger her life, not again.

"No," she replied stubbornly. "I *want* to go. I just don't want to let my family or friends down by not being good enough—"

"You won't," I replied firmly. "You'll be amazing. You always are."

She nudged me.

"Thanks, Ash."

"I would like to say something though, and I want you to listen."

She looked at me, her glance open and willing.

"I'm listening."

"I don't want you to fight today." She opened her mouth to protest, but I continued, "I don't want you in harm's way. What you were saying about GASP is true—you would have had training, and more importantly, you would be supernatural. And you're not. You're very much a human, and breakable. Will you at least consider what I said about the hunt for the jinn?"

I thought she would argue with me, and I prepared for the onslaught. Instead, she wrapped her arms around my waist, leaning her head against my chest.

"I have to do this, Ash."

"No, you don't," I replied desperately. "Everyone would understand—be relieved, even. Hazel too."

"No, I have to do this for *me*. For Benedict, Julian, Hazel and the rest of the kids who were kidnapped from Earth. I lived through all of this... I want to be there at the end."

I kissed the top of her head, smelling the sweet fragrance of her hair. I had half known that my plea wouldn't work, but I had to say it anyway.

"Are you angry?" she asked tentatively.

"No." I smiled. "I didn't expect you to say any different— you're just one frustrating, stubborn lady."

"Who you proposed to." She laughed, prodding me.

"I did. Hence why I want you safe. You're my future. I want to safeguard you as best as I can, so that after all this darkness there will be a light to guide me back."

She held me tighter, not breaking away until I lifted her face gently upward into a kiss.

"Why don't you try it on?" I asked, a little breathlessly a while later.

She grinned.

"Okay, be back in a second."

She picked up the clothes and ran into the bathroom. I didn't hear anything for a long time.

"Ruby?" I called. "Are you all right in there?"

"Yeah," she called back, her voice faint.

I was about to open the door when she stepped back out into the bedroom. Her blonde hair was tied up into a high ponytail, her back straight, her slim but muscled arms complemented by the top and her long legs encased in the black fabric that outlined her taut frame. The outfit was tight, fitting her proportions perfectly.

Wow.

"Um," I stuttered, "you look *amazing*."

"Thanks!" She blushed shyly, giving me a self-conscious twirl.

I wanted to applaud whoever'd made that outfit—maybe send them a handwritten thank you note.

"We should get going," I said reluctantly.

"I'm ready," she replied, squaring her shoulders.

We left the room together, our hands entwined as we made our way back downstairs to meet the rest of the army. I didn't want to let her go.

* * *

Tejus and Hazel were waiting for us at the bottom of the stairwell. Hazel grinned as she laid eyes on Ruby, nodding appreciatively at her outfit, and then glancing down at her own. She was wearing the same get-up, her dagger held in a sheath at her side with another broadsword swung over her back. She held out another sword and dagger to Ruby.

"Here, I got you these."

"Thanks," Ruby replied, hugging her friend. "How are you

feeling?"

"Hungry," replied Hazel, looking guilty and breaking away from the embrace.

"It's a good thing," Ruby replied. "Hopefully we'll bump into Jenus."

"Let's not hope that," Tejus muttered, "not if he's been given powers by the entity—he could actually be dangerous for once in his life."

"Have you and Derek worked out the formation yet?" I asked Tejus. He nodded, focusing in on me, but leaving a hand on the small of Hazel's back. He obviously didn't want her out of his sight. I knew exactly how he felt.

"The dragons and Hawks will lead a small division of ministers on vultures. The rest of them will be joined by the jinni queen and her team as well as the witches and warlocks. Their only job is going to be to try to get close enough to close the portal back up so neither the entity nor his army can escape. The guards will be split into four regiments: one with you, another with me, and then one each with Ben and Derek."

"The villagers?" I asked.

"Staying with the kids," he confirmed.

Good. I didn't want them anywhere near this.

"Jenney too?"

Tejus shook his head. "Jenney's insisting on fighting, Ash."

I grimaced. "Where is she?"

"Outside with the guards. She wants to be in your regiment. But if you want her back here, I can insist on it."

"I'll deal with it," I muttered, moving my way through the crowd and out onto the entrance steps. I scanned the grounds for Jenney, and found her at the far end of the gardens, chatting with some guards.

Furious, I stormed out.

"Jenney!" I yelled once I was close enough. "What in Nevertide's name are you doing?"

She glared at me, color rising in her cheeks. "Ash!"

"Don't 'Ash' me! What are you doing? You're meant to be staying behind with the kids. This is ridiculous!"

"I'm fighting—and you can't stop me."

"I'm EMPEROR, of course I can stop you!" I bellowed.

First Ruby and now this! Why was everyone so eager to go out and meet their death?

"Ash," she replied, trying to keep her tone level and reasonable, "I'm doing this. You can't stop me—really you can't. I deserve a chance to help. These are my people too, you know, and I want to be beside them when we face the entity. It's been great looking after the kids, but now it's time that I did my bit for Nevertide."

I practically growled at her.

She was *impossible.*

"I'll look after her, Emperor Ashbik—on my life," one of

the guards said, stepping forward.

"Me too," replied another.

"And me."

"As will I, on my life."

Four guards knelt before me.

"With your *lives*," I barked, glaring at Jenney, who was looking irritatingly smug. I stormed off, vowing that I'd be watching her throughout the battle. Two people, then, whom I would be constantly worried about as we marched against the entity. It made me feel far from comfortable.

"Did you speak to her?" Tejus asked when I returned to the palace.

"Yes. She's coming with us."

Tejus nodded, looking at me with concern.

"Let's just get going," I snapped.

Derek and Ben met us by the terrace, and we all walked together over to the stables. We mounted the bull-horses in silence, each of us focused on the task that lay ahead.

"Tejus." Derek broke the silence once we'd left the yard. "You lead the first regiment. If there's any sign of it becoming…difficult—please send my granddaughter back."

"You know I will," he replied quietly.

We rode down to the barriers, the armies ready and waiting behind us. Ruby and Hazel trotted up a moment later, followed by the rest of GASP.

"Ready?" Tejus asked me.

I nodded.

"Open the barriers!" he called to the ministers. A split second later they were torn down, leaving the pathway open.

The battle was about to begin.

Tejus

We set off at a quick pace, the bull-horse beneath me quivering with anticipation. I could hear the thundering of hooves behind me and the fast steps of the guards who weren't riding. Just ahead of us, but keeping pace, the vultures, dragons and Hawks soared through the ripped sky.

Hazel rode next to me, but I hadn't forgotten her grandfather's request. The moment it looked like the shadow army might be approaching, she would be sent back. Already I felt wary; the trees either side of us were so still, not even a breeze strong enough to sway the topmost branches. It felt like we were the sole survivors of this land—that there was nothing around us but death and destruction.

I wondered what would happen if we were to fail. Would Nevertide become home to these creatures? A dimension that was nothing more than an empty dark graveyard that bore little resemblance to what it once had been—all evidence of the sentries' time here destroyed completely? And if that was to be the case, would our kind die out and cease to exist?

"Tejus?" Hazel spoke my name, bringing me back to the present. I glanced over at her, seeing concern in her wide eyes.

"Sorry," I replied. I must have looked brooding and tense. "I'm fine," I reassured her. "Are you?"

"Scared, but okay."

"I won't let you be harmed," I promised.

She gave me a small smile. "You can't guarantee that, but I'm not just scared for myself. It's everyone else I'm worried about—you, Benedict, Ruby, Ash, my parents. The list goes on."

I opened my mouth to tell her that she needn't be worried, that she should focus on the task ahead, but I thought better of it. It was too hypocritical given my own thoughts. She would worry anyway, and she would be scared—and there was nothing I could do about it, no matter how much I wished I could.

The main road that ran through Nevertide appeared ahead, and I pulled my bull-horse to a stop.

"It's time for Benedict and the others to leave us," I told

Hazel. She nodded, dismounting from her saddle. I joined her on the ground, and a few moments later we were met by her and Julian's parents, and the small group of humans, jinn and half-Hawk boys that would be going off to find the mysterious jinni—the only creature to ever gain control over our enemy.

I watched as they hugged their children goodbye. It must have been hard for the parents to watch their children leave, not knowing if they'd ever see them again. I had never been overly familiar with such a bond—such easy familiarity between children and parents. My own mother had loved me greatly, but we were royal sentries—there wasn't often the warmth between us that these creatures shared.

Benedict and Hazel were last to say their goodbyes, Hazel's eyes bright with unshed tears.

"Be careful," she told him.

"You too. Remember that you're already a hero for killing Queen Trina, so I figure you can take it easy on this one," Benedict replied.

"Right," Hazel agreed, trying to smile.

To my surprise, Benedict turned to me.

"Tejus, I know you'll look after my sister, but make sure you don't die. You're all right, really, even if you did kidnap us and then turn my sister into a sentry. I'm kind of glad it all happened, so, yeah."

As soon as he finished, he flung himself forward, his small

human arms wrapping around my waist in a brief hug. Not knowing what to do, I gently patted him on the head, looking to Hazel for direction.

She just smiled, delighted.

A moment later he released me, his face slightly pink from embarrassment, and turned on his heel to leave with the others.

"I think I would have been less surprised if he stabbed me," I murmured to Hazel.

She shook her head. "He likes you. He looks up to you."

I doubted that very much, but if it made her happy to believe it, then it was fine with me.

"Let's get going." I turned to the others. The vampires quickly dispersed back into the ranks, Rose's eyes looking bright with unshed tears. Hazel and I returned to our bull-horses. The children and supernaturals quickly vanished off from the path, using the undergrowth for cover till they reached the northern parts of Nevertide, as I'd instructed earlier. The only truly uncharted territory of Nevertide was the Dauoa forest, and the mountain range that lay at the back of it. I had my misgivings about sending the children that way, but had confidence that the Hawks and the jinn would protect them. I really didn't see another way.

We continued the journey, slowing our pace a little as we reached the main road. I felt like we were more exposed here, and though the forests still provided cover on each side of the track, I couldn't escape the feeling that we were being watched.

I glanced over at Hazel, wondering if it was paranoia on my part, or if others could feel it. She was looking out into the depths of the forest on her right, her body rigid.

"Something's coming," she whispered.

"True Sight?" I asked, looking in the same direction. I could see nothing but acres of dense trees, gray tendrils of mist winding their way along the bottom of the forest floor.

"No," she replied, her eyes still fixed in the distance, "just a feeling."

The bull-horses were becoming jumpy too. I scanned the sky over the trees, looking for a shadow looming in the distance, but I saw nothing.

"Let's just keep going," I replied. "It might be because we're approaching the cove. Maybe it knows we're coming."

I steadied my bull-horse, placing a hand on its neck, and then dug in my heels. The pace picked up, and I could hear the army behind me following suit.

Suddenly, the bull-horse reared up, whinnying in fright. Hazel's did the same, and I leaned over to pull hard on the reins. We both came to a standstill. A few moments of silence followed, then I heard the hoofbeats of Ash riding to the front of the line, followed by Derek, Ben and Aiden.

"What's going on?" Derek called.

"I don't know," I replied. There was nothing to indicate why the creatures behaved so oddly—the sensation of being watched remained, but other than that, the land was still.

"I can't see anything," Ash replied, turning his bull-horse around on the path. "Has there been anything—"

He broke off suddenly as we all heard the sound of undergrowth being whipped back—something was headed toward us, moving fast. Before Ash or I had a chance to use True Sight, there was a loud shriek and a creature appeared before us, coming from the left-hand side of the pathway, staggering into the middle of the road.

It was a woman, naked, covered with a thick black liquid the consistency of tar. As I took in the spectacle, I noticed that the tar was seeping from crude rune carvings on her skin.

"Abelle?" Ash whispered.

The apothecary?

She was unrecognizable, her face distorted in sheer terror and rage, her mouth gaping open and her eyes bulging as she stared at us, unblinking, trapped in her own madness.

"The master!" she cried, holding out her hands toward us in a silent plea…for help?

"Oh, my God," Hazel murmured next to me.

"The master is *evil*! Dark! H-He was promised as a benevolent power," she screeched at us. "He LIED! They all *lied*! He is coming for you, and you won't survive. He will DESTROY!"

Her wild eyes met mine. She vomited, black tar spilling from her mouth. Her body spasmed, twitching grotesquely. Then her eyes closed, and she dropped, collapsing into a heap of flesh on the ground.

"Abelle!" Ash cried, leaping toward her.

"Ash," I warned, not wanting him to touch the body.

He ignored me, dropping down next to her.

"Forgive me," he murmured in anguish. "I should have known—I should have stopped you."

"Ash." Ruby approached him slowly. "There's nothing you could have done!"

He looked up at her, his face pale.

"How did I not know about her being an Acolyte? About any of this? I knew her my whole life. I was so sure that she…" He stopped, unwilling to finish the sentence.

"I think she did love you," Ruby replied gently. "She just believed that this was the best thing for Nevertide. She got it wrong."

Ash stood up, his head bowed, almost as if he was ashamed to face us.

The jinni queen moved forward, breaking the ranks. She shook her head sadly at the sentry on the floor. The other two witches and the warlock, Ibrahim, followed.

"This is dark indeed," she whispered, crouching down to get a better look at the seeping runes.

"Do you recognize the symbols on her skin?" Ruby asked.

"No," the jinni replied slowly. "This is not magic I know. But it is dark. She will be grateful for death."

The jinni gently pressed the apothecary's eyes closed.

"Move the body," I murmured to two guards behind me, "we'll bury her later."

They nodded, moving past Ash as he climbed back up onto his bull-horse. The witches retreated behind me.

"I'm sorry, Ash," I stated. I *was* sorry that he felt her death so keenly, but the fact that she had been put out of her misery came as a relief. The jinni queen was right.

He nodded, not really hearing me.

We carried on our march. If the armies had been subdued before, it was even more the case now. I didn't hear so much as a whisper as we rode on, the footsteps behind us heavy and dull.

This wasn't good.

"Ash," I said, breaking the silence, "I know you probably don't want to, but we're nearing the cove and morale is low. Abelle's terrified them. I think you need to say something. Something that will remind them what they're fighting for."

"I think you are the better man to do it," replied Ash.

"I realize you're upset about Abelle—"

"That has nothing to do with it. They're your armies, Tejus. They want to hear from *you*."

I glanced over at him, not understanding his reluctance to

make the speech himself—he was their *emperor*, and until recently I had been the most despised creature in Nevertide.

"Everything's changed," he murmured, smirking, as if he'd read my mind.

In the distance, I could see the curve of the road where the passage to the cove began. It was now or never, and if Ash wouldn't do it, *someone* had to.

"Fine," I snapped. I spun my bull-horse around to face the oncoming men and women who followed our lead. Most of the sentries and guards looked troubled—only GASP seemed to be focused, their experience no doubt lessening the horror of the appearance of Abelle.

"Armies of the six kingdoms," I called out. They all stood to attention, and a thick, anticipatory silence settled over the crowd. I paused. As I'd said to Hazel, words were never my strong point, and years spent focused only on my own selfish needs left me feeling unequipped for rallying the brave men and women that would be fighting by our side. I looked at Hazel. She gazed back at me, not even a flicker of doubt in her eyes. She trusted me. She believed in me.

"I know you are frightened. I know that your homes and your families have been destroyed. I also know that before the entity brought his evil to this land, things were not much better. In a moment, we will march out to the cove, and face our enemy head-on. When we do, don't think of the Nevertide you know now—think of one that *could* be, with a fair and just emperor"—my eyes lighted on Ash—"a queen who will love you, lands to be re-grown and to flourish. Think of that as you fight. Think of that as worth a life. Think of that as your promised victory."

For a split second nothing happened, and then a roar went up. It was deafening, and my first reaction was to think that the entity had arrived, but I realized soon after that it was cheering—weapons held aloft in salute, steel clashing against iron.

The crowd died down. A moment later, the long, drawn-out blow of the battle horn reverberated through the air.

No sooner had the last notes of the horn drifted to silence than dread unfurled in the pit of my stomach. It had come. Like a thundercloud, the shadow moved swiftly over the land from the cove, blocking out the sun.

"A new Nevertide!" Ash bellowed, unsheathing his sword and holding it aloft as we charged toward the darkness.

Hazel

The mass of shadow was upon us so quickly I hardly had a moment to mentally prepare myself. I had been so moved by Tejus's speech, a wave of love and admiration had felt like it was bursting inside of me—only to be doused a moment later by the onslaught of the shadow.

The bull-horses reared, the trees darkened as the black form divided and spread out on all sides of us, trapping us on the path.

"Hold your positions!" Tejus roared at the armies. "Ministers, barrier at the back!"

I turned just in time to see a barrier rise up into the air, only a few feet away from the final line of the army—the jinn and witches were there, as well as some of the fae and the more novice members of GASP. The shadow slid up the wall of the barrier, but it couldn't pass. Now we only had to face an attack on three fronts—all of which were lined with guards and the deadliest members of GASP.

The shadow was thicker than when I'd seen it last. It was no longer just visible on the ground and the bark of the trees, but mist—cloying, dense—creating a veil around us.

"Ride to the back, Hazel," Tejus commanded me forcefully.

"You need me here," I replied, unsheathing my dagger. "The last person to underestimate me was Queen Trina," I reminded him firmly.

Before he could reply, the shadows surged toward us. Tejus attacked, his sword slicing through the gray and black air. As soon as his blade made contact, a body formed from the mist— ashen, gray, with a face that would have looked human if it wasn't for the colorlessness of it. The creature lifted an arm, swiping it through the air. It only gently brushed against Tejus, but his robe tore and the skin on his sword-shoulder shredded.

With a bellow, he lunged at the creature again, sending his blade right through its chest. The creature howled in agony. As soon as Tejus's weapon had made contact, it had glowed with a brilliant white light that seemed to burn it from the inside. A second later, the creature burst into reddened ash, floating up into the air and then vanishing.

Before I could try to make sense of what I'd just seen or feel a sense of triumph that the immortal water had worked, a loud scream erupted. A guard was tossed like a rag doll up into the air, and then almost entirely consumed by the mists.

All around me I could see the shadow growing closer, hear the dying screams of the guards as they were picked off one by one. Even more disturbing were the creatures themselves; every time the shadow approached, a sentry, vampire or werewolf would make contact, either by sword or tearing into the gloom with exposed claws or fangs, revealing the true form of the creatures: their gray bodies, tattered loincloths wrapped around their waists, their eyes black sockets that glared down at us.

"What *are* these things?" Ash yelled, slicing through another ashen body.

"I…have…no…idea," panted Tejus with effort as he swung his blade into the darkness.

Suddenly, the shadow retreated. It crept back into the forest as quickly as it had emerged, lying in wait, wrapped around the trees and bushes, the armies of the entity watching us—waiting for something. We all looked at one another in confusion.

"Witches, jinn – down to the cove!" Tejus called out, knowing that our reprieve would likely be a short one. A group of the jinn, led by Queen Nuriya, along with Ibrahim, Corrine and Mona and a group of ministers, all hurried to the front of the line.

"Take the long route," Tejus commanded, "try and stay out of the shadow's way."

Before they could move, a voice entered my skull.

The armies of the six kingdoms, the voice slurred, as if the name was an insult. It was the entity—the same voice Tejus and I had heard when we were following Benedict in the Hellswan castle. My body froze, my eyes darting ahead in the distance and either side of the forest—where *was* he?

You have met my children, I see. The voice continued, twisting into my brain so that I couldn't shut it out. I looked over to Ash, Tejus and Ruby, double-checking that they were hearing what I was. They were. I could see them growing pale, Tejus glowering with barely repressed fury as the entity once again infiltrated our minds. The witches and jinn had frozen.

You will all die today, at their hands. But you will be written in the history annals of our time...the sentries who lost their lives when they tried to defend a land that wasn't theirs.

Out of the gloom, a figure appeared, walking toward us on the road.

"Jenus?" Tejus exclaimed, his voice a rasping whisper.

The mists cleared slightly, and Jenus stood before us. His eyes were entirely black, just like the creatures we had just fought, but his body was solid and whole. He still wore the robe he'd been wearing in Memenion's dungeons, soiled and filthy.

Look, Tejus of Hellswan. Look at what your brother has given up in his devotion to me, the entity gloated, a low rumble of laughter following his words.

Jenus's mouth didn't move—neither did any part of his body as he stood, staring at us. I realized that there wasn't any of Jenus left, just an animated corpse for the use of the entity. It was revolting, and I turned my face away in disgust.

Before you are all ended, I wanted to tell you who you fight for, the entity continued, *who you follow into battle—blindly being led by men who are just as corrupt as me.*

A vision started to form in my mind, definitely not put there by me.

Is he mind-melding with us?

The vision started to become clearer, showing Ash in the kitchen of Hellswan in his servant's clothing, standing above a pot of liquid, looking around the room before pouring an unmarked vial into the concoction.

Your emperor is an emperor-slayer, the entity hissed.

Next we saw Ash walking with a tray of food, heading for the quarters of the old emperor. I heard mutterings coming from the sentries behind me.

The vision flickered and another replaced it. It was Tejus and I, our first kiss at the banquet—the image playing out in slow motion, our lips meeting, my flushed skin.

The commander of your armies loves only his once-human girl, and will leave this land the moment he gets the chance.

The vision changed again, showing Nevertide, but burnt, broken. Fires raged throughout the forests, the fields scorched, homes and castles nothing but rubble.

This is the Nevertide they promise you. The Nevertide to come. If you fight today, you fight for nothing but ashes and dust.

The visions ended abruptly. Tejus had lunged forward, his blade aimed toward the base of Jenus's throat. Jenus batted the sword aside easily, grabbing Tejus's forearm and causing him to drop the sword. It clattered to the ground. Tejus staggered to the floor, grabbed the blade, and swiped it across Jenus's lower body. Jenus flew back just in time to avoid impact. In my mind I heard the entity laughing.

Tejus rose, this time focusing on the shadows that were starting to re-emerge from the forests. I joined him, holding a broadsword in one hand, my precious dagger in the other.

I glanced back to the armies of Nevertide and GASP. They too were fighting off the approaching shadow, and my mom leaped into the gloom. As she landed, one of the creatures formed, and she buried her mouth in its neck, tearing at the ashen flesh. The white light appeared, and the creature combusted into ash. My great grandpa, Aiden, was wielding two swords at once—not even bothering to use his claws as he annihilated the oncoming shadow, his face fixed in a deadly grimace. Micah and Kira were working as a pair; one leaping up, one attacking down—tearing at the ashen flesh from both ends. Bastien joined them, and soon they were creating a widening circle where the shadow refused to approach, backing away to attack somewhere else.

"Hazel!" Tejus yelled.

I turned to see part of the shadow inches from me. I lunged with my dagger, lifting the blade upward as the creature's face emerged from the mists. A second later, and it was gone. Without any time to think, I began to battle another, faintly repulsed once again by how easily my blade slid in, and astonished by how real the flesh of the creatures seemed to feel, just the same as Queen Trina's.

I could still hear the screams of the guards and ministers, but they weren't as frequent. I glanced over at Tejus. Even in the midst of battle, danger on every side, he was watching me. He smirked, plunging his sword into another member of the entity's army.

"Showoff," I managed, taking out another one.

A roar of fury distracted me suddenly, and I turned to my left, seeing Ruby alone, a little way off from the rest of the army. She was battling one of the creatures, but the shadow was starting to form around her.

"Ruby!" I cried, trying to warn her.

I rushed forward, but Ash got there first—leaping forward toward the gloom that was encroaching on Ruby as she battled.

He swiped his sword once, slicing through one of the creatures, but out of nowhere, the shadow lifted him up—a hand appearing out of the mists and raking though his torso.

"ASH!"

I watched, feeling like the movements of the land and everyone around us had just slowed down. Ash's body twisted in the air, his blood already seeping through his robes, and then landed, crumpled onto the ground.

"ASH!" Ruby screamed.

Ruby

No.

NO!

I dropped to the ground, ignoring the shadows that surrounded us, growing closer by the second.

"Ash?" I rasped.

He looked up at me, and all I became aware of was his warm brown eyes fixed on mine, not betraying pain or fear, but just the same steady look he always gave me that let me know I was loved.

"Ash?" I repeated, praying that he would talk to me—say something so I would know he was going to be okay. I looked down at his body. My throat tightened, and my entire body felt like it was plummeting down into the earth like a dead weight. He was soaked in blood, the opening of his robe revealing the torn flesh beneath his shirt. The cuts were deep.

Too deep.

"Hold on, Ash!" I cried, looking around for something to compress the wounds. He would bleed out if I didn't get him somewhere safe. Not knowing what else to do, I tore off my own top, pressing it against the wound.

"Ash, please speak to me," I begged, keeping one hand compressed on the wounds, the other cradling his head. I kept looking back toward his eyes, making sure they didn't glaze over or flicker shut.

"Sh-Shortie," he croaked, his breath rasping.

I smiled with relief, my own tears running onto my lips. I knew the danger was far from over, but at least he was fully conscious—that was something.

"Ash, Ash. Don't you *dare* die on me, okay?"

Slowly, with a low groan, he moved his hand up to his chest and placed it over mine.

"You and I? We're not finished yet." He smiled.

At his words, I felt a strange sensation in my chest, a dull ache—like my heart was literally ripping inside of me. The thought of losing him suddenly became too much to cope with. I just *couldn't*. I wouldn't go on without him.

I looked up, taking in what was happening around us.

Tejus, Hazel, Derek, Caleb and Aiden were fighting off the shadow—they had surrounded Ash and me, creating a sword-wielding barrier between us and the entity's army.

"We have to get out of here," I whispered to Ash.

I looked back desperately toward the crowded ranks of the army. Every one of them was completely caught up in the fight, especially the witches and jinn. Most of the bull-horses were either being used by battling sentries or had already met the same cruel fate as their riders—but there were a few of them left.

There was one riderless bull-horse, standing in the middle of the path, whinnying in horror as guards, vampires and other supernaturals surrounded it, all battling furiously.

"Ash." I leaned down toward him. "I need to leave you here for a moment, okay? But when I'm gone, you need to keep the pressure on. Can you feel where I'm pressing? You need to do that, okay?"

He nodded, and both of his hands came up and pressed my top against his chest. With a sob, hardly daring to leave him for a second, I ran toward the bull-horse. My small size in comparison with the sentries was for once helpful. I was able to push my way between them without too much trouble.

"Ruby!"

My mom whirled into my path, her expression horrified at my appearance—I realized I was streaked in blood.

"It's Ash!" I cried before she could say anything, screaming at the top of my voice to be heard over the sounds of battle. "I think he's dying. Help me! Please, please, help me!"

She grabbed the reins before I could reach out and touch them, and then wrapped her other arm around my waist, holding me up against her. Barreling sentries and vamps alike out of the way, my mom dragged both the bull-horse and me through to the front of the armies.

Tejus, Derek and the rest of the vampires moved out of the way for us, continuing to hold the shadows back from Ash's body. My vision blurred as I realized that his arms had gone limp—his hands were no longer tight over his chest.

"NO! NO, NO! MOM!" I screamed, rushing toward the ground. She grabbed me, pulling me away from his body.

"Up on the horse, Ruby!" she roared.

"NO!"

"LISTEN TO ME—up on the horse!"

My mother bent over Ash's body, picking him up in her arms as best she could and carrying him over to the bull-horse. I scrambled up on the saddle, ready to take him.

"To the immortal waters," she breathed, "it might help. Don't stop."

She handed me his body, and I sat him up in front of me. He was out, stone cold. But I could feel the slight palpitation of his heart as his back rested against my chest. There was still hope.

"Look after yourself," my mom yelled furiously from the ground.

I nodded, spurring the terrified bull-horse into action with a sharp kick. It reared up, and I unsheathed my sword, ready to fly through the black mass.

They would not touch me.

In this moment I was invincible, the enemy nothing more than it had first appeared—shadows and dust.

The bull-horse leapt into the gloom, and I swiped my arm tirelessly, moving faster than I thought was possible. A scream tore from my lungs. It echoed in the gloom, my battle cry— my voice in the darkness that promised vengeance and pain to those who might stop me.

We rode harder, the faces of the dead men appearing like a tunnel either side of me as I ran my sword though them like butter. Their ashes flew into my screaming mouth, choking me with their bitter burn.

Soon the gloom cleared. The wisps of dawn could just be made out in the east. I rode on, dust flying behind us, my breath coming in short, heavy gasps as I willed the creature on faster. I would not lose him. I would not lose everything I had.

We're not finished yet, I silently returned his oath to him.

We're not finished yet.

TEJUS

My men were dying.

Ash's still body, lying in Ruby's mother's arms, wouldn't leave my mind. I fought with an anger and ferocity I hadn't known I possessed. The energy to carry on, wielding my sword although my arm felt numb and dead, came from the sentries around me—taking and giving our power to one another as we continued our fight.

It wasn't enough.

From the moment that Ash's body had been flung up into the air, we had stopped gaining the upper hand. The guards and ministers were shaken—badly. We were moving back, the army backing away from the steadily seeping shadow. The screams of the guards grew more constant, and though the deadly supernatural creatures who made up GASP fought with as much ferocity as I'd hoped, they couldn't hold back the threat. No matter how many of the entity's soldiers we killed, the shadow continued to grow, showing no sign of its mass ever retreating or shrinking.

"We need to retreat!" I called over to Ben as I took another aimless swipe into the black gloom.

"Agreed," he yelled back, decapitating another of the creatures. "I'll get the witches on it. Why the hell won't these things stop *coming*?"

"We need to get more barriers up!" I called, hoping that there would be enough sentries and witches nearby to help. At the moment I was surrounded by a team of vampires, who had all gathered to the front, where the force of the shadow seemed the strongest – but I needed sentries now, and the witches, to maintain a barrier that might just keep the rest of us alive till they could get out of here.

Don't go yet.

I lowered my sword for a moment, taken aback at hearing the entity's voice again. I'd thought it had left its armies to finish us off.

That battle isn't won. Would you let your people go on to suffer another day?

I tried to ignore it, continuing to battle the strange, ashen creatures that appeared out of the mist. But if the entity was trying to persuade us to stay, I knew it meant we were lost—we couldn't keep losing our fighters at the rate we were going.

"BARRIERS!" I called again, and this time ministers, witches and jinn all broke through the ranks. Standing either side of me, they tried to form a barrier strong enough to hold off the shadow.

Each time the flickering, translucent wall began to form, the gloom would run up against it, dragging it back down. The ministers started to try to syphon whoever was nearest. Hazel stumbled forward, too worn out to be sucked dry of her energy.

"Rose! Caleb!" I called to her parents, not knowing where they were—I couldn't take my eyes off the shadow still growing in front of me in case I faltered. "Take her back—she needs to get away from here."

I stood in front of Hazel, making sure she came to no harm. Ben joined me, and we created a two-man barrier in front of her.

"I'm okay," she objected weakly. "I can still fight!"

I took a step back, letting Ben handle the shadow for a few moments while I got her to safety.

"Hazel, you're too weak, you need to get back!" I replied, my throat constricting as I saw how pale she was. It was an effort for her to remain standing up.

"Caleb! Rose!" I called again, and this time was relieved to see Caleb rushing toward us. He pulled Hazel up into his arms.

"Thank you, Tejus," he replied. "I'll get her to safety."

I grabbed on to his arm before he carried her back to the end of the line.

"If things get worse, can you use a witch to get her back to the castle? You'll need to take a minister with you as well."

"We can, don't worry." He nodded his agreement, forcing his way through the crowd. I saw Rose join them, and together they made their way swiftly toward the back of the ranks.

I turned my direction back to the shadow. Ben was fighting on, standing next to Derek and Aiden. I joined them, relieved to know that Hazel was in safer hands than mine.

"We need more ministers!" I called out. "Get the barriers up!"

Brother, why so eager to shut me out?

"SILENCE!" I cried out, sick of the entity's voice invading my mind.

"Tejus!" Derek called, pointing at something through the gloom. A few moments later, my brother reappeared. He was smiling, a slow, evil grin spreading across his face as I swung my blade furiously at the oncoming creatures.

"Hold the shadow back!" I called to the vampires, slashing my way toward the body of my brother.

You wish to face me alone, brave soldier of Hellswan?

"I wish to watch you die," I spat.

So, vengeful Tejus, do you not see how your brother loved me so much he gave up his very soul to serve me?

At the mention of my brother, I raised the sword above my head, bringing it down with as much force as I could muster. Before it could come into contact with his skull, Jenus reached up and caught the blade in his grip. He held it still, his hand like a vice as I struggled to pull it away.

I gave him strength.

He released the sword and I yanked it back, my muscles trembling. I swiped again, this time aiming for his neck. Once again, he caught the sword in his hand—not an ounce of blood bleeding from his body, not a wince as the blade bit into his flesh.

I gave him speed.

Once again, he let me take the sword, and I staggered backward. I turned quickly to fight back the shadow that had started to pool around me, killing three of the entity's creatures in one motion. Then, with a battle cry, I leapt forward—the tip of my sword aiming for his chest. Just before I came into contact with his skin, the blade was once again caught—held easily in both his palms, as if he were at prayer.

I gave him new life.

This time, I was the first to release the sword, taking a dagger from my belt. Derek, Ben and Aiden appeared out of the mist, cutting through the shadow as they both launched themselves toward Jenus. Derek leapt toward him, aiming for his throat, but Jenus batted him backward. His body was flung into the gloom. Ben roared, running at full speed toward Jenus, a sword in either hand.

Child of the fae, your fight will come later.

The entity laughed, batting away Ben's advances as it had done mine. Derek returned from the mist and gloom to see his son being knocked back on the floor, and rushed once again at the entity. He slammed into him, the force sounding like great boulders collapsing in an avalanche, but still my brother just laughed.

Three of the dragons started circling above, coming from the forest where they'd been trying to ambush the shadow from the rear. Their claws reached down, trying to get a grip on Jenus. When that failed, they scorched the air—great balls of red-hot fire blasting from their mouths. Jenus was engulfed completely, his form disappearing behind the licks of flame. Before I could even hope that this meant victory, Jenus stepped forward again. His body blistering and burnt, but alive. The shadow hadn't abated.

"We need to retreat!" I shouted. The flames didn't even look like they'd weakened him. Either the entity was invincible, or we needed to find another method of destroying it. Force wasn't going to help.

"Retreat!" Ben echoed my call, and I heard it going up

behind us—the guards and ministers and GASP calling it out.

We had been defeated.

"Take them and go!" I yelled to Derek. "Get out of here. Head for the castle."

"Follow my lead!" Derek called out to the guards. "Don't be far behind," the man called to me as he departed. I nodded, telling Ben and Aiden to join him. They would have fought alongside me till the end, but Hazel was going to survive this battle and I needed all the force in Nevertide to protect her in the coming days. I heard the growls of reluctance from some of the fighters and guards that refused to go, and then the sudden silence as the witches vanished most of the army.

Once they had left, I backed away from Jenus. My fast-draining strength and my dagger were the only things I had to protect the few ministers and GASP members who had refused to leave my side.

Jenus smiled at me, taking a step forward.

It was the end.

I could feel the shadow drawing in.

Suddenly, a wall of flame shot up before me. It was white and cold, instantly chilling the sweat that dripped off my brow. Before I could speak, the jinni queen appeared.

"Ice flames. More potent than even dragon fire." She smiled. "Let us hope it buys us some time."

The ministers started to build a barrier to contain the

shadow, and I could feel them draining the last ounces of energy away from me. I raised my arms to help fortify it, relieved to see that the shadow was shrinking back from the flame.

Then Jenus stepped out of the fire.

His blisters were now frozen and dusted with ice, but still his figure remained upright, seemingly unbothered by the attack.

After all this time, do you think the tricks of the jinni would frighten me?

He stepped closer, running a finger down the barrier. It rippled slightly, showing just how flimsy it was against his power. He laughed.

"Run!" I cried to the rest of them. Perhaps I could hold him off long enough to allow the rest to get far enough away.

"I won't leave you," replied Nuriya.

"You will. They *need* you!" I urged.

She exhaled, lowering her eyelids for a brief moment. "Then we will never forget you, Tejus of Hellswan." A second later, she was gone.

Alone again, then. Is it bravery, or foolishness, Tejus? Or is your self-hatred so great that you might willingly give up your life just for a chance to escape yourself?

The barrier shook again. I tried to maintain it as best as I could, but I had moments or less till it collapsed completely.

"I do it for her," I whispered, "that she might have a chance."

"TEJUS! TEJUS!"

A familiar voice screamed out my name.

"Hazel, NO!"

Jenus smiled slowly. I turned to glance at her; she was running toward me, her eyes wild and panicked.

"Get back!" I bellowed at her, wondering how the hell she'd managed to escape her parents and the witches —and suddenly terrified.

"No!" she panted. "I won't leave you!"

She held her dagger aloft, her eyes fixed on Jenus.

I tried to sink all my strength into the barrier, willing it to hold. As Hazel ran the last few paces toward us, I reached out to hold her back. My hand clasped onto her arm. In the next moment, I dropped my dagger as a force surged through me— it was so strong, so altering that I almost thought Jenus had killed me without my realizing.

A white light shot up around us, blinding me. As the force persisted, I felt Hazel's energy flowing into mine. Growing it, making it unbelievably strong. As my eyes adjusted to the light, I realized it was coming from the barrier, the power of our connection solidifying it in a way I'd never seen before—it blazed brightly across the pathway and along the sides of the forest, sending the shadow back.

"What *is* that?" Hazel gasped. I glanced at her, her dark hair and clothes bleached by the light. She looked like an avenging angel—a creature come to offer me salvation in my darkest hour.

"I think it's you," I whispered.

"I think it's *us*," she replied, looking up at me with the same reverence I felt.

"Now we run," I commanded, dragging her with me as I turned toward the empty road. I didn't want to wait and see if the barrier would hold against the entity. As we sped past the walls of white light on either side of us, the power continued to surge through us both. I looked ahead. The blaze continued for as far as I could see, lighting our way home.

SHERUS

Most of the sentries and GASP members had been vanished by the witches. Lidera and I had thinned ourselves so that we were invisible, but I didn't want to leave without making sure that the jinni queen was safe. I could see her floating next to Tejus, and then the sight of ice fires blasting upward. I wanted to drag her back, to get her out of here, but it wasn't my place.

During the battle there had been so much confusion, so many wounded and bleeding that the smell of iron infiltrated my nostrils, the fighting army taking on a surreal, nightmarish quality that all too well matched the omens I'd experienced back in the In-Between.

Is this the end? I wondered.

I looked in the direction of the cove. There were gray shapes, like thunderclouds, forming on the horizon just above where the portal stood.

What are these creatures?

I had never faced anything like them before…I had never heard of an army that could move like the mists of nature, and then become the shadows of men—their features fleshy and real, but the color of ash and darkness.

Hazel, Derek's grandchild, ran past me.

Before I could stop her, my sister placed a firm hand on my arm.

"Sherus!" Lidera commanded. "We need to leave!"

The shadow was moving closer. To my relief, I now couldn't see a sign of Nuriya. She must have already traveled back to the palace. Only Tejus and Hazel remained. Foolish girl.

I needed to move. I turned on my heel, dragging my horrified eyes away from the portal and the creatures that surrounded it. My heart froze as I wondered if I was witnessing the entity and its shadow pouring out into the other dimensions. Had we truly lost all hope?

Then I stumbled, my footing lost as I became suddenly blinded by a brilliant white light. Hastily I staggered up, Lidera and I looking about in confusion as either side of the path became walled by the light. It was the same barrier I had seen the sentries create, but stronger… purer.

"Sherus!" Lidera cried again. "For the sake of the gods, if you want to live to see the dawn, MOVE!"

I ran, not turning back again. I feared none of us might live to see the dawn.

READY FOR THE FINAL BOOK
OF "SEASON 5"?!

Dear Shaddict,

I hope you enjoyed A Throne of Fire!

The next book, <u>*ASOV 41: **A Tide of War***</u>, is the thrilling **FINAL** book in what has been "Season 5" of the *A Shade of Vampire* series!

A Tide of War releases <u>**March 20th, 2017**</u>.

Visit <u>www.bellaforrest.net</u> for details on ordering your copy.

Check out the epic cover!

Thank you so much for continuing this journey with me.

I will see you again soon, back in The Shade…

Love,
Bella xxx

P.S. Join my VIP email list and I'll send you a personal reminder as soon as I have a new book out. Visit here to sign up: www.forrestbooks.com
(Your email will be kept 100% private and you can unsubscribe at any time.)

P.P.S. Follow The Shade on Instagram and check out some of the beautiful graphics: @ashadeofvampire

You can also come say hi on Facebook:
www.facebook.com/AShadeOfVampire
And Twitter: @ashadeofvampire

Made in the USA
San Bernardino, CA
16 October 2017